Tessa'

~ West S. ~
Tessa & Lucas
© 2016 Jill Sanders

Follow Jill online at:
Jill@JillSanders.com
Web: http://JillSanders.com
Twitter: @JillMSanders
Facebook: JillSandersBooks
Sign up for Jill's Newsletter @ JillSanders.com

Summary

Geeky teen pushover Tracy Bracey is finally dead, replaced by the beautiful and confident Tessa. After years of bullying, the darkness hovering over her appears to be fading. She has at long last become the vibrant woman she truly wants to be. Well, there is one thing missing… But with a promising music career taking off, the last thing she needs is the incessant matchmakers in town trying to hook her up with every wannabe cowboy available.

Lucas James is hot as hell, but the cloud of mystery surrounding him is so thick, you can cut it. Who is this guy and where did he come from, anyway? He seems nice enough, but you definitely wouldn't want to mess with him. How does a guy like this come to land in sleepy Fairplay, Texas? Is he running from something or someone? Whatever it is, he's not talking.

Lucas just wants to be left alone to deal with his past, but now a sexy brunette songwriter thinks she has the answers to all his problems… Unlikely! But, at least she might be a pleasant distraction.

Books in the West Series by Jill Sanders

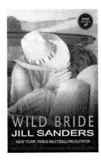 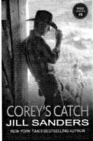 

Other books by Jill Sanders

The Pride Series

The Secret Series

The West Series

The Grayton Series

Last Resort
Someday Beach
Rip Current
In Too Deep
Swept Away

Lucky Series
Unlucky In Love
Sweet Resolve

Silver Cove Series
Silver Lining

For a complete list of books: http://jillsanders.com

Tessa's Turn

by

Jill Sanders

Chapter One

Tessa couldn't believe what was happening. Her eyes filled as they lowered her mother's small casket into the ground. Its pure white color contrasted with the East Texas red clay dirt that she'd always hated. Even though her mother had been sick for several months, nothing could have prepared Tessa for the loss. Not even the new friends she'd made in her hometown of Fairplay, Texas, could ease her pain.

They were all here to support her today. Savannah and Billy stood the closest, each of them holding a sleepy child in their arms. Maggie was closing in on five, while Audrey was just coming up on her first birthday. Both of the girls were dressed in dark gray dresses that Tessa had helped her friend put on them earlier that day. They

9

matched their mama perfectly, in every way.

The West clan was close behind her. She could hear a couple of the younger boys ask their daddies when they could take off their "church clothes" and have some pie. No doubt, their mothers had baked plenty of pies for the reception that was happening shortly after the burial.

Tessa's eyes moved back to the simple white box and sighed. Her father's fingers brushed hers and she reached out to take his hand. When had it gotten so frail? When had her parents grown so very old?

She glanced over at him and saw him wipe tears from his eyes with his white handkerchief. Carl and Leslie Keys had been in their late forties when Tessa had come along. She'd been the surprise of their lives and, according to them, a blessing.

She supposed that, if they had been younger, she would have had a better chance at things. Her love for her parents had never wavered, but she'd still dreamed of a family full of children with parents young enough to enjoy them and hip enough to help her through her troubles.

She glanced over at her father and smiled when he wrapped an arm around her shoulders.

"Your mother was so happy to spend the last few weeks with you," he said softly.

"I should have come home sooner."

He shook his head. "You did right, finishing the

semester. She would have wanted that."

A tear slid down her face. Her father reached up and, with a shaky hand, wiped it away gently just as the preacher finished talking.

"The Keyses would like to invite everyone out to their house for a luncheon to honor Leslie's wonderful life. If you need directions, I have a printout." He waved a small stack of paper's Tessa had printed out on her father's computer.

"How are you doing?" Savannah asked while shifting Audrey in her arms.

"Good. Do you want me to take her?" Her fingers itched to get ahold of the baby again. Savannah must have guessed it because she gently moved her sleeping daughter into her waiting arms. The baby felt good snuggled up next to her. Even with the added heat, Tessa felt a little more centered.

"I hate the circumstances, but I'm thankful to have you back in town." Savannah smiled over at her while she brushed a finger down her daughter's dark head.

"I'm not…" She bit her lip and nodded. She didn't want to admit to her friend that she wasn't sure how long she planned on staying. She knew she needed to be here for her father, but just being back in Fairplay, Texas, unsettled her stomach.

She stood next to her father, holding Audrey as everyone passed them with words of

11

encouragement. Then she handed the baby back to Savannah and made her way towards her father's sedan to drive him home.

"You don't have to stay in town on my accord," her father broke in less than a mile away from the church. She glanced quickly over at him.

"What does that mean?" she asked, turning her eyes back towards the road.

He took a deep breath. "I know how you feel about the people in town. Well, most of them. Anyway, I don't want you to feel obligated…"

She stopped him by reaching over and taking his hand. "Dad, I'm where I need to be right now. I'm no longer a little girl, afraid of what others think of me."

"I can see how much you've changed." He smiled and patted her hand. "You're no longer our little Theresa."

She cringed at the old-fashioned name she'd always tried to hide.

"No, I'm Tessa now." She smiled and squeezed his hand.

"Tessa," he sighed. "Much better than Tracy." He nodded. "God knows why they started calling you that." He glanced out the window and retreated into his own thoughts.

Tessa knew why they'd called her Tracy. Knew exactly who had called her that and remembered the day that Tracy had died, the day she'd jumped from the bridge.

***

What the hell was everyone doing in town? Lucas cursed under his breath. It seemed like every damn car within fifty miles was blocking him from a good meal. Of course, he wouldn't be so damn hungry if he'd remembered to stop by the grocery store last night on his way home from Tyler.

It didn't matter anyway, since he doubted the Grocery Stop would have been open at midnight. Laying on the horn, he stopped himself from flipping the bird to the car blocking him as he jumped the curb and pulled into the parking lot at Mama's, one of the only decent places to get a meal in town.

Then he did curse as he read the sign on the door. "Closed, in honor of Leslie Keys. If you're hungry, come on down…" There was an address in bold black.

Well, shit. He turned back towards all the cars and felt his gut turn. It was a funeral procession.

Resting his head back, he decided he was one of the worst sons of bitches in town. Who swerved in and out of a funeral procession because they had missed breakfast and lunch?

He pulled his truck into reverse and decided to try the Grocery Stop for a cold sandwich. He sighed when he saw the same note on their door.

Damn! That was the problem with living in a small town. The whole place closed down when someone died or got married.

Deciding he'd rather spend a lifetime sitting on hot coals than an hour with a bunch of strangers, he started to pull out of the parking lot, only to realize that there was a string of cars driving down the wrong side of the road. What beat it all was that they were all following the sheriff's car.

It was like one big parade, blocking his way to any food. He watched several cars drive by slowly and realized that there was one source of food in town. And it was free. All he had to do was get in and out before anyone stopped to ask him questions.

Making up his mind, he pulled in behind a white Jeep and followed everyone slowly out of town.

The house wasn't big, but it was well maintained. It sat almost two miles out of town near the old railroad tracks. There was parking in the large front yard, so he pulled in next to the Jeep and waited until everyone got out before opening his door.

He felt his stomach growl and almost hunched over with pain. It had been almost twenty-four hours since he'd last shoved something in his mouth. Why the hell hadn't he planned better?

He followed the stream of people walking up

the wide front porch stairs and was thankful there wasn't anyone standing at the door to greet guests.

It was too crowded in the living room to make out anything short of the fact that the walls were painted a nice cream color and the paintings that hung around the room were something he'd expect to see on his grandmother's walls.

The furniture was pushed aside to make more room for people, and there were a ton of them standing around, chatting. Some, he noticed after a while, were coming out of the back room with full plates in their hands. His stomach led him towards the wonderful smells and he noticed a rather large black woman, whom he only knew as Mama, scooping out baked beans onto plates.

"Hmmm, thawt I'd see you here," she said with a rich Louisiana accent as she frowned slightly. She smiled when she heard his stomach growl loudly.

"It's where the food is," he said, grabbing up a plate of baked beans and holding it out for her to load up with the cooked brisket and pork.

"Dat it is." She nodded. "You be good and pay your respects to Miss Leslie's family." She nodded towards the corner of the room and he glanced over where an older gentleman was sitting at the end of a large dining room table.

He turned back towards Mama and frowned. "I'm just here because you closed down—"

15

She bopped him on the back of the knuckles lightly and shook her head. "Don't make me crawl over dat table." She crossed her arms over her rather large chest and glared at him.

Finally, he sighed and nodded. "Fair enough." He glanced down at the plate, then back up at her. "Is that corn bread?"

She chuckled and put two large slices on his plate.

Since there was an empty spot at the table, he decided to head over and "pay his respects," while he shoveled food into his gut.

When he sat down, a young woman shifted next to him and glanced his way. She had a full plate of food, but had yet to touch any of it.

"Something wrong with the food?" he asked, taking a large bite of the juicy meat.

"No," she said, pushing the plate farther away from her. "I'm just not hungry." She shifted slightly away from him again.

"Well, if you're not going to..." He nodded towards her plate.

"Help yourself." She pushed the plate towards him and moved to get up.

"There you are." A busty blonde rushed towards the table. "I was worried sick..." She stopped when she noticed him shoveling the brunette's food onto his plate. "Well, really!" She crossed her arms over her chest and turned to the brunette. "You need to eat!" She pulled the plate from his grasp and set it back in front of the brunette, all while giving him a glare of death.

"Savannah, I'm not hungry," the brunette said softly.

"I've spent all day with you and I know for a fact that you've only had two mints." She glared at him again as he continued to shovel food into his mouth. His stomach was beginning to feel normal and he was sure he was over the worst part of the hunger pains. "Promise me you'll try to eat something." She turned away from him.

The pretty brunette nodded and reached for her fork. "Only if you can convince my father to eat something as well." She nodded towards the old man at the head of the table.

He realized that she was family and felt bad for trying to take her food.

"I'm working on it. Worse case, I send Jamella in here." The blonde chuckled, then turned. "Oh! That's one of mine crying." She turned to go, but then stopped and met his eyes. "Don't take that plate from her until half of it is gone." She waited until he nodded in agreement.

When the woman disappeared down the hall, the brunette pushed the plate back towards him. "If you don't tell her, I won't."

He shook his head and pushed it back. "Eat," he

said between bites.

She leaned back and sighed. "There might be a whole pie in it for you, if you tell her I ate half."

"What kind of pie?" he asked, finishing up his plate.

"Blueberry." She took a sip of her tea, making him realize he hadn't gotten a glass for himself.

He thought about it and almost took her offer.

"You should eat. I'm sure your..." He let his words hang.

"Mother. Leslie was my mother."

His eyebrows shot up a little as he looked over at the older man.

"I'm sure your mother wouldn't want you to starve yourself on her account."

"I'm hardly starving," she said, crossing her arms over her chest.

No, he thought, not starving. Her coloring also told him that she wasn't on the verge of passing out from lack of food. But she shouldn't go around avoiding meals either.

Then his mind switched gears from food to how wonderful it would be to have the pretty brunette curled up next to his side.

"At least have some of the corn bread. It's delicious." He handed her the bread from her plate and set the rest in front of him. "It's a deal breaker." His eyebrows lifted when she started to set it aside. "Don't make me go get Jamella." He waited and watched her brown eyes move back towards the kitchen area to where Mama was still scooping up food.

"You play dirty," she said under her breath, then took a bite of the bread. When her eyes closed with pleasure, he knew she'd finish the entire piece off without another word.

"I'm sorry about your mother." There, he thought, my duty is done. He'd just finished everything on her plate and finally felt like his stomach was borderline full. But the promise of pie had him pushing that feeling aside.

"Thank you," she said taking another sip of her tea. "Did you know her?"

"I don't think so." He frowned over at her father as he too pushed an almost full plate aside. Unlike his daughter, the old man looked like he was about to fall over if he didn't get some food in him. "Looks like your dad might need some persuading to eat." He nodded to the end of the table. Before she could reply, Mama walked into the room and sat down next to him.

"I know you goin' to finish dat whole plate," she said, setting her plate down next to his and pushing his back in front of him. "Besides, if'n you don't, you won't get a piece of my blackberry pie I baked special for ya."

19

"Now, Jamella…" the older man started.

But Jamella huffed and crossed her arms over her chest.

"I think Mama has it under control," the brunette whispered back to him. "I'll go get your pie. I'm sure you're anxious to get out of here."

"What makes you think that?" he asked.

The left side of her mouth curved up. "You've looked towards the front door at least a dozen times since sitting down. You haven't once relaxed back in that chair, and you've been tapping your foot incessantly."

He immediately stopped. "It's a nervous tic."

She nodded. "I'll meet you out front with it. I'm going to have to sneak it out the back way."

After she left, Jamella glanced up at him and nodded. He figured he had her permission to vacate the building, so he started to make his way towards the front, grateful that everyone seemed too busy in their own conversations and food to bother with him.

He stood out on the front porch for less than a minute before the brunette walked around with a pie covered in tinfoil.

"There's a piece missing, but since you forced the bread down me, you'll just have to make do."

He nodded and reached for the pie. "Thanks."

"Have you lived in town long?" she asked, throwing him off balance slightly. "I only ask… well, it didn't seem like you knew anyone here."

He shrugged. "Almost a year. I don't."

"Why not?" she asked and then bit her bottom lip. His eyes followed the motion and he felt his mouth water.

"I tend to stick to myself." He itched to get out of there.

"I didn't mean to make you nervous." Her dark eyes looked shadowed, like she'd spent too many nights without sleep. Sad, but curious.

"You don't." His eyes moved towards the front door. "They do." When his eyes moved back to hers, he thought he saw understanding in them.

"I didn't get your name," she said, turning back towards him.

"Luke," he answered quickly, using his nickname. "I didn't get yours, either."

"Tessa." She glanced back towards the front door when a loud baby cry came from inside. "Thank you for stopping by." She turned to walk inside, but he stopped her.

"I'm sorry about your mother," he said, again.

She nodded slightly and then disappeared through the front screen door.

As he drove away, he couldn't get her soft

21

brown eyes out of his mind. For the first time since moving to Fairplay, he thought he'd finally met someone who could understand the pain he'd gone through. Maybe it hadn't been such a bad choice to move to the middle of nowhere after all.

Chapter Two

*W*hen Tessa stepped back into the house, she felt a wave of exhaustion roll over her. She supposed it was the hunger that she'd avoided, but still, she doubted her stomach could handle anything more than the corn bread and the slice of blueberry pie she'd saved for herself later.

"There you are." Haley West walked over and took her arm. "We were looking all over for you."

She was pulled into her mother's sewing room, which was crammed with women all holding sleeping babies. Her mother had a large, soft sofa across the back wall that she'd often taken naps on while working on her latest quilt.

"We wanted to ask you something," Haley said, shutting the door softly behind her.

"This isn't an intervention, is it?" she joked but they just stared blankly at her and looked worried. "Listen, I'm thankful—"

"Oh, sit down," Savannah added quickly. "Give us a chance to spit it out first." Her friend walked over and took her arm, then pushed her into her mother's high-back desk chair.

"Okay." She stretched the word out as she looked around the room.

"We want to know what's up with you," Alexis, Haley's older sister, blurted out. Alex never shied away from anything, but the fact that her face was a little flushed told Tessa that she was uncomfortable.

"Up?" she asked as she leaned back.

"Are you going to stay in town?" Savannah asked.

"I haven't really decided that yet."

"Well, how long are you going to stay?" Savannah shifted the sleeping baby in her arms.

"I'm not sure. Why?" Her eyes narrowed as she looked around the room. "You aren't looking for a babysitter, are you?" She'd spent a lot of her high school days babysitting some of their older kids. She'd loved every minute of it, but didn't think she could handle it at the moment.

Several of them laughed. "No, of course not. We have each other, and then you'd have to fight

24

the grandparents off."

"What's this all about?" She crossed her arms over her chest.

"We miss you," Savannah added, only to gain a glare from Tessa. "Oh, okay, we were trying to figure out what we could do to convince you to stick around. After all, your father really could use you. And we *do* miss you," she repeated.

She looked once more around the room at the group of ladies. Most of them were a good five years older than Tessa, some even more. Every last one was happily married and had kids or one on the way. She glanced down at Holly's growing belly and felt an emptiness that hadn't been there before. Then it hit her—her mother wouldn't be around to enjoy her grandchildren. She'd never get to share those tender moments from daughter to mother. Nor would she be present for her wedding, something they had always dreamed about together.

"Oh, we've done it now." Haley rushed over to her and wrapped her arms around her. "We didn't mean to make you cry."

Tessa felt more arms around her. "It's just…" She didn't want to tell them that she was jealous. Jealous of their lives, of the path they were all taking.

Why was she flooded with all these emotions? Glancing around, she remembered that the West sisters had lost their mother long before and that their father was gone as well. Shaking off the bad mood, she straightened her shoulders.

She was done being depressed. Done letting her emotions get the better of her. That's why she'd changed her name, her career, her life. She wasn't scraggly little Tracy anymore! She was beautiful, strong Tessa with a promising music career ahead of her. When she'd left Houston, she'd had three agents fighting to sign her

"It's not your fault. I guess I'm just a little more tired than I thought." She stood up. "I haven't made up my mind about staying more than a month. After that"—she glanced around— "I'll let you ladies know."

"That's all we could hope for." Savannah stood back up. "Now, sit back down and tell us all about your music career while Haley gets you a slice of pie and ice cream."

Tessa sighed as she sat back down. "I don't know what you want to hear."

"You can start by telling us why you changed your name." Savannah walked over and sat on the edge of the sofa as she handed the sleeping Audrey over to her.

Tessa smiled down at the baby in her arms. "Because Tracy is gone." She kept her eyes down.

"Tessa suits you better," Savannah said, shocking her.

"I agree. I mean, your full name is Theresa, right?" Holly asked.

"Yes, it was my grandmother's name."

"It's kind of old-fashioned. You could have gone so many different directions. How did you start going by Tracy to begin with?"

She sighed and closed her eyes. Just hearing the name brought back all the hurt and pain.

"I think they started calling me Tracy in grade school, the first time I had to have braces." The room was silent.

"Kids can be so cruel," Savannah added, only to have all eyes turn on her. "What?" She sighed. "I should know, I used to be the biggest jerk of them all." Everyone started laughing as Savannah smiled. "Maybe I should change my name? I mean, I'm no longer the person I used to be."

"True," Alex added. "What?" she said when all eyes moved to her. "Oh, don't get me started. Everyone in this room knows how I used to feel about her, but now"—she smiled over to her friend— "I rather like the new Hanna."

Savannah groaned, then said. "Okay, no new names for me." Everyone chuckled.

"So, have you found an agent yet?" Alex asked.

"I have several who want to sign me. I'm just waiting for the last one to give me an offer."

"Wow, that's amazing," Holly added.

"Yes, now Fairplay has a world-class author and a singer," Haley said as she walked over and set a large plate next to Tessa. She reached down and took Audrey from Tessa's arms. "Eat." She nodded to the pie and ice cream. "Before it melts."

"I'm not really that great of a singer," she added.

Alex made a noise, causing everyone to look at her. "I heard you sing at your high school graduation. Girl, you can belt it out amazingly."

"Not like you," Tessa added. "Everyone within three counties comes to the Rusty Rail to hear you and Grant sing together." She sighed as did everyone else in the room. The duo was almost legendary.

"I did find a good man." She smiled back at her. "And he does have a great voice."

"If I could find someone like Grant to sing with, I think I'd have a better shot at things." She frowned into her melting ice cream and pie.

"Well, you can't be doing too bad. You've got three agents duking it out for you," Savannah said.

"What they want more than anything is access to my songs so they can produce them." She glanced around the room.

"I don't get it?" Holly added.

"I sent them each a tape, and several songs I'd written. They liked the tape, they loved the songs.

They want to hire me to write songs for some of the top country singers or find an artist to record them."

"Like who?" Haley asked.

"Well, I'm not sure. One agent talked about Carrie Underwood." Everyone gasped. "But, I'm not sure if that's true or not."

"What about Faith Hill?" Alex added.

For the next couple of minutes, the room was filled with voices as the ladies around her speculated about all the famous singers Tessa could be writing for. She sat back and before she knew it, had finished off the whole plate of pie and ice cream and was feeling a little better.

"I'd love to hear some of your songs," Alex finally said when the chatter died down. "We can try them out at the Rusty Rail, if you want?"

"I'd like that," she added. "I have a few songs I'd like to try out with a couple singing."

"I know it might be too soon… after losing your mother, but how about next week? Thursday?"

Tessa nodded slightly. "We can meet before, so you can go over the lyrics."

"How about you shoot them to me in an email. Grant and I will work on them beforehand."

She forced herself to remain calm and not bite her bottom lip, something the old her would have done. Panicked. Instead, she dipped her head in

29

acknowledgement and jotted down Alex's email address on one of her mother's sticky notes.

"Are you going to be staying with your dad?" Savannah asked.

"I'd planned on it. Why?" she asked.

"Our renter in the house downtown just moved out last week and the place is sitting empty. You can have it for as long as you want it."

"I couldn't..." she started.

"Yes, you can. We'll rest easier knowing someone is there looking out for the place. Besides, our insurance won't let the place sit empty for too long. You'd really be helping us out."

"I..." She looked around and realized that part of the problem with being home was this house. She felt like her old self staying in her small room with the pink flowered wallpaper. "I might take you up on the offer. But I probably should stick around here for a few days." She glanced towards the door.

"Take your time. I'll tell Billy we can stop looking for a new renter. If you need anything before then..."

Everyone else in the room chimed in, offering their help. When the group finally joined the rest of the guests out in the main rooms, Tessa felt a little more stable. She even grabbed a plate of cold meat and beans and heated them up.

When she found her father a few minutes later, he was looking exhausted. She pulled Lauren West aside and asked if she could help clear the house so her father could get some rest.

Less than fifteen minutes later, the place was cleaned and emptied.

"You didn't have to shoo everyone off so quickly," her father said, still resting in his large recliner.

"I was feeling pretty tired and wanted the quiet," she fibbed as she sat next to him in her mother's matching recliner. "How are you doing?" She reached over and took his hand in hers.

"I'm missing your mother." His voice was soft. "But I'm dealing. How about you?"

"The same." She leaned her head back in the chair.

"I'm glad you're home," he said.

She couldn't get her voice to work. Part of her was glad she was there for him, but the bigger part of her wished more than anything to be somewhere else. Anywhere else. She didn't want the memories, the hurt and shame of being back in Fairplay. At least not until she had everything she'd ever wanted in life. After the talk with the other ladies today, she realized there was still an empty spot she needed to fill.

***

Luke finally made it to the grocery store the next day. He'd been thankful for the pie later that night when his stomach had rumbled again. He'd also wished for a gallon of ice cream to go along with it, but he wasn't going to be too picky.

He wasn't one of those people who walked into the store with a list or, for that matter, even an agenda. All he had was a growling stomach and a pocket full of cash. Needless to say, he'd filled his cart until it had almost overflowed. Then he'd loaded everything into the back of his truck and headed home, all without a single word muttered.

The dark-haired clerk had chatted the entire time she'd rung him up, but he'd just listened and nodded when she asked him a question. He felt their relationship had grown. The first week after he'd moved to Fairplay, she'd asked him too many questions, and he'd just silently looked back at her. She'd finally understood that he wasn't a talker, and happily chatted enough for the both of them.

He was just pulling out of the parking lot when he spotted the local vet walking out of his office. He pulled the truck over and rolled down his window.

"Hey, doc," he called out. The man glanced over and nodded, then walked towards his truck.

"How's it going? You're Lucas, right?" Luke had already forgotten the man's name even though he'd heard it a dozen times in town and felt pretty bad, so he cleared his throat and nodded.

"I can't complain, but one of my heifers is having a problem chewing. Looks like she's got something stuck in her mouth."

"I can swing by and take a look at her after lunch today. If you'll be around."

He nodded again. "Thanks." He started to roll up his window, but the man's hand on his truck stopped him.

"I didn't get a chance to talk to you yesterday at the Keys' place." Luke waited. "We've got a new bull that's ready to stud, if you're interested."

He thought about it. "I heard that McDowell's stud is one of the best around."

"True enough, but this year, our blue ribbon calf has come into season. He won two years in a row. You can come out and take a look at him sometime if you want."

Luke nodded. "Sounds good. I'll see you after lunch." As he drove away, he glanced back and remembered the man's name. Chase Graham. He and his father ran the vet clinic. He also remembered running into his pretty brunette wife a few times in the grocery store. She and her sisters had tried to get him to show up for the Fourth of July event they'd thrown down at the town hall, but he'd been too busy putting up a new fence to stop and have tea with a group of ladies.

When he pulled onto the dirt lane just down from his place, he stopped. There, in the middle of the road, was a small bundle of fur. He was too far away to know what it was or if it was still alive.

He was the only one who traveled up and down the road, so he'd most likely hit it on his way to the store that morning. The guilt ate at him.

Throwing his truck into park, he got out and started walking slowly towards the fur ball. He stopped when he heard a low growl.

"Good to know that I didn't kill you," he said softly, walking around until he finally saw the brown eyes looking back at him. The small Boston terrier was so skinny; he could see every rib. Not to mention, the poor thing's fur was matted down with dark blood.

"Easy..." He approached the dog, only to stop when he heard a low whine. He walked back to his truck and grabbed his work coat from the back seat. Then he walked up behind the dog and swooped in quickly, covering its head and sharp teeth before he could get bit.

The dog whined a lot, but didn't put up too much of a fight. "Looks like the vet will have a lot more to look at when he gets here." He bundled the dog up, set it in the seat next to him, and drove towards his barn rather than his house. Putting the groceries away would just have to wait a few minutes until after he got this one settled into one of the empty stalls.

It took a little more time than he'd imagined,

since he wanted to make sure the little guy or gal wouldn't escape, so he'd had to secured the stall as well as put out some fresh water.

His first instinct was to feed the poor creature, but if the dog needed to get a shot, maybe it was better on an empty stomach? He figured either way that the water would have to do for now.

After unloading his groceries, he made himself a quick sandwich and then sat on his small front porch to enjoy his food. The ice tea he'd made last night felt good as he looked around his small ranch.

He'd come here a little over seven months ago to start over. More like escape his problems. All the hurt and guilt he'd felt after the accident. He hadn't guessed that he'd be bringing most of it with him, or that it would boil up from the inside out. Still, he thought as he looked around, it was better to wallow alone than have everyone he knew hound him about opening up about it.

He'd spent the last few months steering clear of anyone who tried to find out more about him.

Where had he come from? Why had he chosen Fairplay? Was he married? What did he do for a living? Did he have family? All questions he'd learned how to avoid.

He planned on becoming a part of the town someday, but for now, he just wanted his space and the quiet that came with it.

After finishing off his sandwich, he walked back out to the barn to check up on the dog. It had drunk a little of the water and curled up to his jacket and was fast asleep. He'd gotten a better look at the thing and realized that the dried blood was from a small cut on his hind leg. There was a tear in its hide about a quarter of an inch thick and deep. It looked like it had gotten caught on a barbed wire fence somewhere.

At least he could stop feeling guilty for hitting it. Still, it would probably need stitches and a new home. He'd been thinking about getting a few dogs. Bigger ones, though. He frowned down at the small dog laying in the hay on his jacket. He needed dogs that could rustle up the cattle and be strong and fast enough to stick with him on a ride. Not one of those damn lap dogs ladies like to hide away in their purses.

Just then he heard a horn honk outside and walked out to see the vet's truck drive up.

Waving, he pulled his hat down lower over his eyes to shield the sun.

"Howdy," Chase called out as he reached out his hand. "I don't think I've properly introduced myself. I'm Chase Graham."

He nodded. "Yeah, I've heard your name around town. Lucas James, but I go by Luke."

"Well, of course everyone in town is talking about how you snatched up this place from the bank. Haven't had any problems with it so far?"

He turned to glace back at the small house.

"No, the water heater could stand to be replaced, but so far so good."

"So," Chase turned back towards him. "Where's this heifer of yours?"

"Well, I ran into a small issue on the way home I'm hoping you can help me with..." He nodded towards the barn door. "Seems the little guy ran into a barbed fence." Chase followed him into the barn and back towards the stall. When he opened the door, the dog rushed towards them, tail wagging and tongue drooling.

"Well lookee here." Chase bent down and snatched up the dog. "Mighty scrawny critter," he said as he ran his hands over him. "She'll need some stitches for the cut. That and a few pounds of fat on her should do the trick." The dog leaned up and started licking Chase's face. "Plus a whole slew of shots..." He glanced at him. "If you're looking to keep her?"

Luke thought about it. "Do you know anyone in town that lost a dog?"

"Nope, but I can tell you the pound is pretty full. I can take her to the clinic, patch her up, and hold her for a few days until you decide. Either way, I'll want to keep her overnight after the stitches and shots."

He nodded as his fingers reached out and

scratched the small dog under her chin. He was rewarded with a quick lick and a snuggle.

"Looks like she likes you." Chase chuckled. He handed the dog over to him and Luke instantly fell for the stupid mutt.

"Patch her up, let me know when she's ready, and I'll come get her."

Chase nodded. "My wife and her sisters are dying to know what brought you to Fairplay," he said out of the blue.

"Found a good deal on the ranch," he answered, wanting to keep his answers short. He'd come up with excuses and reasons for everything and had been prepared.

"No matter to me, it's just..." Chase rolled his shoulders. "You know how women can be. If I didn't ask the next question, I'd be eating out in the barn with the horses tonight." He took a deep breath.

"Shoot," Luke said, handing the dog back over to him.

"Well, they want you to come to dinner sometime."

"They?" he asked, feeling his gut twist.

"My wife and her sisters, along with our families. Wes and Haley are your nearest neighbors. They own the place just above yours." He nodded towards the west. Luke knew the place he was talking about.

"The cop?"

Chase nodded. "Alex and Grant live closer to Saddleback, that's our place."

"I've heard of it. Driven by a few times as well," he added, leaning back against the stall door.

"Well, we'd like to invite you out this weekend. We're having a barbeque. It's our daughter Abbi's birthday."

Luke watched as the man's chest puffed out slightly.

"I'm not—"

"Don't say no yet. Just think about it. You're welcome anyway. We start the party around eleven on Saturday." He sighed and Luke thought he looked relieved that task was over with. He shifted the dog under his arm. "Since her bleeding has stopped for now, let's leave her be while I take a look at that heifer of yours."

Chapter Three

There were too many little kids running around the yard to count. The noise was almost deafening, but Tessa was enjoying every minute of watching them play.

The birthday girl, for her part, wasn't dressed in a frilly dress, but instead had on jeans, a flannel shirt, and well-worn pink and brown cowgirl boots. She was chasing a bigger boy who had a hat on with a pair of foam bull horns taped to the top. Several kids had small ropes and were trying to catch him like a steer. It was quite amusing to watch.

It had been almost a week since she'd buried her mother and still the emptiness had yet to subside. She doubted it ever would. But, she had to admit, being around all the kids was helping a lot.

Still, it was getting harder to fight the depression that came with being home. She'd avoided going into town since returning and had only been seen publicly at her mother's services. Even then, she'd spent most of her time locked up with what she deemed her only friends.

The bitterness and hurt ran deep. Not to mention the feeling of shame she carried around inside. Even though the truth of her "accident" had never been discovered, she still carried the guilt.

She had never confided in anyone, not even her mother, about what she'd done that day on the bridge. Nor did she think she ever could.

"Are you okay?" Lauren asked, sitting down next to her on the front porch swing.

"Sure." She plastered on a smile. "I'm just enjoying watching the kids play."

Lauren looked off towards the yard where several of the men were encouraging the kids to hog-tie the teenager they had just roped. Neither could hold in a chuckle as the teenager reared his head up and gave his best impression of a cow mooing.

"It can be a farm around here in more ways than one," she said and turned towards Tessa. "You looked sad just a moment ago. Thinking about your mother?"

"Some." She took a deep cleansing breath. "I

still can't believe she's gone."

"I know what you mean. After losing our parents…" She shook her head slightly. "Let's just say, if you need someone to talk to…"

They both glanced over as a silver truck bumped up the lane, spewing dust in the air. They turned back towards each other when it stopped and parked.

"You know you can talk to any of us. We've only got one another now, but sometimes all you need is the ear of a friend." She reached over and patted her hand gently.

Just then it hit her—what she would have done years ago to have someone to listen to her when she was going through hell at school. She'd spent so many years feeling alone and like an outcast, she didn't even really remember not feeling that way.

"Thanks." Tessa felt her stomach settle a little when she knew Lauren wouldn't push her farther. Then they both glanced over to the yard. "So, what's the story for tall, dark, and brooding?" She nodded towards Luke, who was walking towards the group of men standing in the front yard. She didn't want to admit it to Lauren, but she had wanted to tag "sexy as hell" on to her description.

"No one really knows anything about him other than his name. Lucas James. His name fits him. I imagine a lone cowboy, riding the plains." When

Tessa chuckled, Lauren shook her head. "Sorry." Too many romance novels. Alex lent me a few a couple weeks ago. Anyway, he bought the place down on Cedar a few months back. He sticks to himself for the most part." Lauren turned towards her. "Why do you want to know more about him?"

Tessa shrugged. "He was at the house after my mother's services. He seemed nice enough." She watched as he glanced around while talking with Chase. When his eyes landed on her, she thought she saw recognition, but then he shifted until his back was towards her as Chase pointed out something to him in the distance.

She liked the look of him, but didn't dare hint at the attraction. She'd learned early on in life to keep her secrets to herself. Not that she didn't trust Lauren or her sisters, she just didn't think she could deal with the hurt if it went farther than them.

"What does he do for a living?" she asked, taking a sip of her ice tea, just as Alex, Haley, and Missy walked out onto the porch, carrying large trays of sandwiches, chips, potato salad, watermelon, and drinks.

"Well, as far as we know, he's a rancher," Lauren said as she pushed off, setting the swing moving.

"Oh, who are we talking about?" Alex asked. She glanced around and saw the newcomer. "Oooh, tall, dark, and sexy?"

"Hey." Haley slapped her sister's shoulder. "You are a married woman."

"Sure, but that doesn't stop me from admiring a sexy cowboy when I see one. Besides, Grant is sexier." She smiled and set the tray down on the table.

"Not to mention a lot friendlier," Missy added. "Do you know, I bumped into him a few weeks back at the Grocery Stop and the man didn't say a word to me."

"Maybe he's just shy," Tessa added. Her eyes ran over his back as he talked with Chase and the other men. "He doesn't seem to have a problem now."

"Hmm," Missy said, crossing her arms over her chest. "Maybe he's just stuck up. After all, I heard from Betty who heard it from—"

Haley groaned, stopping the long string of "heard it from, who heard it froms."

"Okay, anyway," Missy said continuing. "Someone heard that he was from a pretty wealthy family in Austin."

"He doesn't strike me as a snob," Alex said sitting back and taking a bite out of her sandwich. "And I've known a lot of snobs in my time."

"Savannah no longer counts," Lauren said as she took a few sandwiches and cut them in half for her kids.

"She does too. After all she did to us when we were younger." She watched Alex shiver, then smiled. "You have to admit, no one in town would have ever expected her to turn out the way she has."

"She was my first friend," Tessa added, then blushed slightly when everyone turned they eyes towards her.

"Your first? Surely you had friends your own age in school?"

She was saved from answering when a pack of kids rushed onto the porch and started devouring the food, which was almost gone by the time the men finally made it up to the porch.

She had wanted to know what else Missy had heard about Luke, but figured the gossip wasn't a reliable source. After all, she'd spent most of her life fighting against gossip about her.

"Hey," Luke said when he sat across from her on the porch. Most of the kids had come and gone, devouring the food quickly so they could continue playing in the yard.

"Hi." She took another drink of her tea to cool off from the heat his eyes were causing her. "I didn't expect to see you here." She wished that she'd spent a few more minutes on her makeup and clothing before coming over. She shook her head at her concern. Ever since her first weeks of college, she'd made sure never to step outside without looking her best. That was one of the lessons she desperately wished she'd learned earlier on in life.

"I wasn't going to, but Chase invited me." He glanced down at the plate in front of him.

If she didn't know any better, she would have sworn he was trying to figure out how to leave already.

"Besides, I figured it was high time I started imbedding myself in the town." He took a drink of his tea, then glanced quickly around. "What about you?"

"Me?" She felt her stomach roll as she thought about imbedding herself back into Fairplay. She felt all the blood leave her face as she thought about going through her entire childhood again.

***

"Woah, I didn't mean to scare you." He set the almost empty plate down and leaned closer to her. "I just thought…" He shook his head and felt like kicking himself.

It really had been too long since he'd been social. He was out of practice. Especially since the last two events he'd gone to, he'd ended up only talking to one person. His eyes moved over Tessa's face again. He wondered why he was drawn to opening his mouth around her.

Everyone else was still standing or sitting on the wide front porch, but for some reason, he felt like they had been abandoned to be alone with one another. Almost like it had been planned.

When he'd first arrived to the ranch, he'd listened to Chase talk about how he'd fixed up Saddleback. How much time, money, and effort had gone into saving the place. Looking around now, he couldn't imagine it being anything short of spectacular like it was now. Still, it had been nice hearing how much the man had done to rescue the place.

His mind had gone over everything he'd already done for his own place and, more important, how much still needed to be done. Which made him think about Tessa. He'd been thinking about her ever since their talk the week before.

"You didn't scare me." The corner of her lip curled up. "It's the thought of moving back to Fairplay full time that scares me."

His eyebrows shot up in question. "Didn't have a good childhood here?"

She chuckled and rolled her shoulders. "You could say something like that."

He set his tea down and glanced around. There were half a dozen kids running around in the front yard. Most of the women and men had followed them out to the yard now and were enjoying watching a young boy ride an older-looking horse in the corral.

Ever since eight months ago, he'd shied away

from crowds.

"How about a walk?" he blurted out.

Her dark eyebrows shot up in question.

"I…" He swallowed. "I'm not good around a lot of people."

"How about to the barn and back?" She pushed her plate aside and he noticed that she'd only eaten half her sandwich. There were a couple of dogs laying on the front porch and when she got up, she tossed them each part of her sandwich.

"Lauren said that you might use Roger as your stud?" she said when they stepped off the porch.

"Roger?" He almost lost his footing as she giggled.

"One thing you need to understand about the Wests. If Alex gets to name an animal, it's going to have a human name."

He held in a chuckle. "I suppose news spreads fast in a town this size."

"Then you're from the city?" she asked, keeping her eyes towards the ground as she moved.

His gut took a punch. "Yeah, Austin."

She glanced at him. "Originally?"

He nodded. "I moved around some, but I was there for the most part until I moved here. You?"

She shook her head. "Born and raised here until I went to school in Austin a few years back."

"What did you major in?"

"Arts. Music to be precise." He noticed her shoulders straighten slightly with pride.

"Really? That's pretty cool."

"You?" She stopped in front of the large red barn and leaned against the post of the corral.

"After joining the military, I didn't really have time for school." He propped a boot up on the lowest rung and watched the kid ride the horse. Actually, he was impressed with how well he was doing, like he'd been born in a saddle.

"Do you ride?" She nodded towards the kid.

"Not as well as he does." He chuckled.

"That's Ricky. Chase and Lauren's boy. All the Wests are born for the saddle." She sighed and rested her elbows on the post. "When I was younger I wished I could run away and be in the rodeo."

He turned slightly towards her. "Not the circus?"

She shook her head. "I'm afraid of clowns."

He smiled. "Who isn't?"

"I know, right?" She turned towards him. "I wanted to be the girl who sang the national anthem at every event."

"So, you must have a pretty great singing voice then?"

She sighed. "It's okay." He frowned until she added. "I get by. Really, it's my love for writing music that sets me aside."

"Oh?" He leaned closer, and when his arm brushed hers, he froze. Just the slight feeling made him realize how close they were. He swallowed the lump in his throat and leaned slightly back as she continued to chat about the possibility of getting signed with an agent.

The entire time she talked, memories flooded his mind of another woman. A pretty petite blonde with haunting green eyes. One whose laugh was warm and rich. Whose slightest touch had made his entire body shake.

Then, before he could stop it, the other memories where filling his mind. Screaming, bright lights, and then all the pain washed over him. He felt his breath hitch, his chest tightened, and his palms turn sweaty. Instantly, his flight instincts kicked in.

"I'm..." He broke in and dropped his foot as he took a step back. "I'm sorry, I... I just remembered I have some hay being delivered. I've got to go." He turned without another word and rushed to his car.

By the time he pulled into his driveway, his breathing was back under control. Closing his eyes, he rested his head back and tried not to think about how much he'd embarrassed himself.

Wasn't this why he kept to himself? He had hoped that he would have everything under control by now, but today proved to him that he didn't.

He felt stupid for making a fool of himself in front of Tessa. He didn't know why her opinion of him mattered so much, but out of all the people in town, hers did. He thought about stopping by later that week to apologize, but just the thought of facing her again made his heart beat out of his chest.

Best leave it be. After all, if the rumors around town were true, she wasn't going to be sticking around much longer anyway.

Chapter Four

It had been almost two months since her mother had died and Tessa was getting frustrated. Why the hell was she still in Fairplay? Especially since she'd penned a deal with the Harper Group, one of the largest and best known talent agencies and publishers in the south She had sent them three songs so far, the three that Alex and Grant had tried out at the Rusty Rail, each one a bigger hit than the one before. She had a book full of other songs that she wanted to work through, but there was so much she still had to do.

In the last few weeks, her father's health had deteriorated, both physically and mentally. Every day she tried to get him up and out of the house to work on chores. Her parents hadn't owned a lot of animals, but still, the two horses and roughly a dozen cattle needed daily attention. Not to mention the several dozen chickens that still lived in the coop out back. The place was falling in on itself and needed a new metal roof, which meant hiring someone to do it since she didn't want to see her frail father up on a ladder.

She could do things herself, but the last time she was up on a roof, she'd broken two fingers and had to be carried down the ladder, fireman style. Boy, that had been embarrassing.

Thinking about it reminded her how awkward of a teen she had been. Not only a klutz, but nerdy too. Because her parents had been older, she'd been raised almost as if she'd been from a different era. She'd watched a movie once where a kid had been raised in a bunker by his folks, who had believed a nuclear war had actually taken place. When he'd emerged, he'd been so far out of his element, kids had made fun of him. Tracy had been that kind of teen.

But that time was over, so naturally she talked herself into climbing up the ladder while her father watched, giving directions. They had gone into town and purchased all the metal sheets and screws needed to replace the roof.

"Once you get the old metal down, I can—"

"No." All morning long she'd been fighting with him about staying off the ladder. "You're keeping both feet on the ground." She glared at him. "Besides, there isn't that much to do. It's not like our chickens have a luxury mansion." She chuckled as she tossed another piece of the old metal down, and he went inside to get out of the heat.

She was wearing her father's thick gloves to keep from banging up her fingers this time. Even though it was almost a hundred degrees out, she was wearing a pair of her father's long overalls with a long-sleeved shirt and steel-toed boots. There was no way she was going to end up in the clinic this time.

She was just tossing the last piece of metal down into the yard when a white truck pulled into the drive. Instantly, everything shifted inside her. She wished more than anything that she'd gone in to shower and was sitting on the front porch in a flowing white dress with her hair and makeup firmly in place.

Why did Luke always come around when she least expected? She quickly glanced down at her attire and groaned. She thought about ducking behind the back side of the coop until he left, but he stepped out of the truck and waved in her direction.

"What in the hell are you doing up there?" He rushed towards her, a sexy frown marring his lips.

"Replacing the roof on the chicken coop." She decided to act cool and continued scraping off the remaining metal chunks.

She was so focused on her task; she hadn't heard him climb the ladder. She stopped herself from squealing when his hands wrapped around her waist and lifted her up.

"Why in the hell are *you* the one doing this?" he growled next to her ear as he pulled her towards the ladder.

"Let go." She pushed his hands away from her, scared she would fall.

"Not until you're safely back on the ground." He hoisted her up and easily carried her down the ladder, much like she'd been carted off the last roof she'd been on.

When her feet hit the ground, she reached up and pushed him, hard, on the chest. He didn't budge. Instead, he smiled.

She reached up and pushed a strand of her sweaty hair out of her eyes and then stuck her hands on her hips. "Who do you think you are? Coming onto my land, tossing me around?" She took a step closer to him. "You have no right…"

His smile just continued, so she started back up the ladder to finish her job.

"Oh no, you don't." His hands once more covered her waist. "If it needs to get done, hire someone." He picked her up once more and moved between her and the coop.

"I can't afford to. Now would you kindly move."

"Then I'll do it," he said as he started rolling up his sleeves.

"The hell you will." She crossed her arms over her chest and frowned at him. "If you think—"

He stopped her by just touching her arm. "Tessa, what kind of friend would I be if I let you climb back up there and you ended up getting hurt." He finished rolling up his sleeves. "You can hand me up the new stuff." He nodded towards the pile of sheet metal. She *had* been wondering how she was going to get it up the ladder all by herself. "All you have to do is hand them up to me." He tucked the cordless drill under his arm and climbed the ladder. "Here," he said once he'd made it up. "Like this." He waited until she maneuvered a piece to the side and held it up on its tall end. He easily reached down and took the piece from her bare-handed.

"My father has more work gloves." She quickly retrieved the extra pair and tossed them up to him. "You don't have to do this, you know."

"Sure I do," he said between securing the screws in. He glanced down at her. "I owe you an apology for bugging out on you like I did at the birthday party. I've already apologized to Chase and Lauren for skipping out."

She stood back and watched him work, trying hard not to drool. "It was probably my fault. I can't even remember what I said that had you running."

He chuckled and took the next piece of metal from her. "Nothing. Sometimes my mind just snaps to the wrong things." He shrugged. "Like I have PTSD." He moved and secured the next piece of metal.

"Were you in the service?" she asked.

"Special Forces for a few years. I got out early late year." So many things about him fell into place. He fell silent while he worked. He secured three more pieces before talking again. "I guess that's part of the problem."

"What is?" she asked, rolling her neck to get a better look at him. He moved to the edge and smiled down at her.

"I have a hard time opening up. Or so they told me."

"Oh?" She felt her heart kick when his brown eyes met hers. She waited for him to continue.

"I guess I'm just worried about too many things." He waited as he pulled up the next piece. At the rate they were going, they would be done in less than an hour.

"What kind of things?" she asked, curious.

"This and that. My feelings and thoughts, I suppose."

She bit back so many questions she wanted to ask him. "Why do you think that you are afraid to open up?" He shook his head and she noticed his eyes had grown dark. "You don't have to tell me," she added quickly.

"You sound just like my shrink." He stooped and glanced at her. "Sounds like you've been to one too." When she just continued to look up at him, he sighed and turned back to his task. "I might tell you, maybe some other time..." He took the next-to-last piece. "If you've decided to stick around Fairplay."

She was thankful she was bending down to pick up the last piece of metal, so he didn't see the blood leave her face. "I haven't decided, yet," she lied.

"Why the aversion towards the town?"

She held the metal, waiting, while he secured the last piece.

"Not the town, directly. Just some of the people in it. They are the reason I went to counseling."

His dark eyebrows shot up as he reached for the last piece of metal. "Everyone I've met so far seems pretty nice."

"Oh, I'm sure they are. But you've only met a few."

He nodded. "True enough, but I can't imagine damning an entire town for a handful of misfits." He glanced down at her, then back to his task. "Besides, school kids can be so cruel. Most of them grow out of it once they start their own families or move away."

59

She laughed. "Some don't."

He finished up and climbed back down the ladder as she held it steady for him. The way his jeans hugged him had her heart rate spiking. She mentally decided it had been way too long since her last date.

When he got down from the ladder, he swiped at the sweat on his forehead and smiled at her. "You know, I probably was one of "*those*" kids in school."

"Oh?" She doubted it. After all, the man had just spent almost an hour up on the roof of her chicken coop in almost a hundred-degree weather, all because he didn't want her to get hurt. A man like that, she just couldn't imagine making fun of a girl because she wore braces or had stringy hair and wore outdated outfits.

"Sure, I mean, I was captain of the basketball team, I played quarterback in football, then, after graduation, I entered the forces and was head of my unit. I got engaged to the head cheerleader…"

He stopped all movement as he quickly retreated into his mind. She noticed the change in him right away. He lost a few shades of coloring and his dark eyes focused on something far away. He was so deep in his mind that she doubted anything or anyone could reach.

Moving closer, she touched his arm. He jumped slightly and blinked a few too many times.

"Are you okay?" she asked. When he just nodded his head and opened and closed his mouth a few times, she felt bad for him.

"I'm a terrible host. Here you are, working and sweating in the heat and I haven't even offered you a glass of tea yet." She took a step back, then turned around quickly. "I'll be right back." She rushed towards the house, not wanting to take a chance to glance around and see if he was still there.

She walked into the house and rushed up the stairs and into her room to change out of the overalls. Pulling on a pair of shorts and a tank top, she desperately wished for a shower, but knew there wasn't enough time. Instead, she sprayed herself a few times with her favorite perfume and double-checked her hair and face in the mirror.

Then she rushed downstairs and pulled the pitcher of tea out along with two glasses and made her way back outside.

She was surprised to find him sitting on the front porch swing. It looked like he'd cooled off some and was enjoying the cool breeze coming from the hills.

"You've got a nice place here," he said once she set the pitcher and glasses down.

"It's always been my favorite thing about Fairplay." She sat next to him and poured them both some tea. "What brought you into town?" she

61

asked as she handed him his glass.

"I suppose the same thing that brings others to a small rural town in Texas." He leaned back after taking a long drink from the tea. "Peace and quiet."

She couldn't hold in the sarcastic chuckle.

"What?" he asked, turning slightly towards her.

"You don't move to a small town in Texas for peace and quiet."

"No?" He looked amused.

"No. Small towns in Texas are full of scandals, gossip, and politics."

"Oh?" He reached down and poured himself some more tea.

"Sure. I guess you weren't here when the mayor's wife almost shot and killed Grant, or when the tornado ripped through, destroying half of the town. Or when there was a drug gang that burned down half the hillside, or the other time the drug cartel came into town and..." She stopped and shook her head. "Needless to say, Fairplay has had its fair share of excitement."

"I guess so." He smiled. "Then again, anywhere you go... things happen." He sighed and rested back, his eyes moving over the chicken coop. "I think they like it." He nodded to the chickens who were busy pecking around the yard. Some of them had already wandered into the building to check things out.

"Yup, beats getting rained on."

"So…" He reached up and set his glass down. "What else needs to be done around here?"

***

He didn't know what had caused him to ask the question, but something was drawing him to help her. He knew how fragile her father was and doubted he was able to do most things around the place that needed to get done.

He chalked it up to just being friendly, but the truth was, he liked being around her. She was really the only person he'd met in Fairplay that he felt completely comfortable around. The funny thing was, he wasn't quite sure why.

It had taken him a long time to build up the courage to come apologize for his actions. He'd talked himself out of it over a dozen times. But he'd run into Chase at the grocery store and had to admit that he needed closure with Tessa before she moved away. That was, if she was going to leave, something everyone in town was still speculating about.

She had avoided answering his questions. For some reason, he desperately wanted to know the answer.

He'd heard at the store that she'd been signed with an agent and that her music was being highly sought after by a few big-name artists. The list he'd heard was most impressive, but kept changing and growing every time he heard it. He wondered what she was doing hanging around a town she obviously hated so much.

Still, he'd felt guilty enough to help her with the roof and to ask her if she needed any more help around the place. He'd been avoiding women, in particular, since the accident. He didn't believe that, one day, he would be able to move on, even though everyone close to him had said it would happen, eventually.

All the shrinks in the world couldn't lift the humongous guilt from him. Nor did he want them to. No, he deserved to spend the rest of his days alone.

Tessa had tried to convince him that she could handle anything else that needed to be done around the place, and had accepted his apology for running off on her at the party.

After her father had come out on the porch, Luke had made a quick retreat back to his house. He was becoming very comfortable in his seclusion, something he'd never really experienced before moving to Fairplay.

His life had been full of so many friends and family members that he'd never felt lonely before. Now, as he looked back on his childhood, he knew it had been too full. He'd never taken the time to turn inward and think about what he wanted. Who he was.

His father had molded him from a young age to be who he wanted. Sports were his priority during school. After graduation, the weight of the knowledge that, once his father retired, he would be handed a multi-billion-dollar company had caused him to disobey his father and join the military.

He'd gone straight off to basic, thinking he'd pissed off his old man. But when he returned, his father couldn't have been more proud of his decision. Almost like he'd planned it all along.

He cringed as he thought about going back to that kind of life, where he couldn't be himself or follow his own dreams. He glanced around his small farm and couldn't hold back the smile.

This is what he was meant to do. This is where he truly belonged. Not in some high rise, sitting behind a mahogany desk, balancing so many other's lives in his hands.

Hell, he'd even gotten a dog. Chase had convinced him to stop by and pick up the little one from his clinic. Now, the little girl was settled in his place like she belonged there. He still hadn't picked out a name for her, but was liking the name Lucky, since he'd been lucky not to squash the poor thing in the first place.

Here, he could wake up and do what he wanted every day and the only one that mattered was himself.

Chapter Five

Tessa wanted to rip out her hair. She was sitting at a crowded Mama's, trying to work on her latest song, and instead was staring at a blank screen. Where there used to be a fountain of words that flowed from her, now, there was complete and utter silence in her mind.

Why?

What was going on with her? She glanced around the room and her eyes narrowed. It had to be this town. These people.

Sure, there were a few people sitting in the diner that she considered friends, but the others… She hid a shiver and leaned back.

She glanced over her laptop towards the couple in the next booth. Todd Wellington and Heather Snider were two of the reasons she wanted to vacate Fairplay as soon as possible.

Her eyes moved over to the table across the room where Christy and Stephany sat huddled together, giggling about one thing or another.

The two girls were thing one and thing two in Tessa's book of reasons her life growing up in town had sucked.

There had been plenty of reasons why they had made fun of her growing up. In elementary school she had talked with a slight lisp because of her teeth. She'd been thrilled and excited to finally get braces, but they had started calling her Tracy Bracy and making fun of her metal mouth and guards.

After two years, they removed the braces and it was her clothing that had been too big or too old-fashioned. In junior high, she'd had to have the braces on once more. Her hair had gone through this greasy stage, which hadn't helped at all.

She supposed a lot of what she'd gone through was her own fault. She'd never really had a female role model to look up to. At least not until she'd met Savannah on the bridge that one day. The day she'd first thought about jumping.

"What are you doing?" someone asked, causing her to jump slightly.

She blinked a few times as her eyes focused on another reason she'd hated going to school. John Drake stood next to her booth, smiling down at her.

"Working." She turned back to her screen, only to feel him slide in next to her in the booth, blocking her in. She moved over until her shoulder pushed up against the window.

His chuckle was soft, causing her teeth to clench. It was hard to believe that at one point that laugh would had turned her knees weak and caused her stomach to flutter.

"Looks like you're not getting very far." His arm came around her and his fingers started playing with her hair. She leaned up slightly to get away.

"It's a little too loud in here." She glanced around, wishing more than anything that Mama was working. Instead, there were two ladies she didn't know rushing around like they were late for everything. "I think I'll try to head—"

"Oh, don't go just yet." He started rubbing her shoulders and she felt shivers run down her arms. Her mind whirled to what she would have given in her youth to be sitting in a booth with Johnny Drake's arm wrapped around her like this. "We're just getting reacquainted. I've heard so much about you lately. Heard you're writing songs for Garth Brooks now. You've come a long way from Tracy Bracy." His eyes ran up and down her, making her almost gag.

Tessa held in a laugh. The rumors were being

spun and had weaved their way to every ear in town. Most of them, as usual, were untrue.

"You shouldn't believe everything you hear." She shut her computer down, slid it into its case, and glared at him. "I'd like to go now."

Instead of moving away, he moved closer. She could smell the beer on his breath and cringed. It was only eleven in the morning and he appeared drunk already.

He'd really fallen far from his quarterback and prom king status from a few years back. Her eyes moved over his face. Not only were his once-sexy blue eyes bloodshot, he had a few pimples on his nose and his blonde hair was greasy and pushed back under a hat that looked like it hadn't been taken off in a few years.

What had she ever seen in a boy like this? Just because he'd been the most popular boy in school and was able to get any cheerleader he wanted didn't make him a good person.

Which had been the best lesson Tessa had ever learned.

"I think the lady wants you to leave her alone." The voice was smooth, but had enough firmness to it that there was no mistake that Luke meant business.

John glanced up and chuckled. "I think this is none of your business, buddy." He turned back towards her, his fingers once more reaching towards her, and she pulled away just as they tangled in her hair.

By the time she had said, "Ouch," John was no longer sitting next to her. Instead, he was pulled up close to Luke so their noses were practically touching.

"You're leaving now," he softly growled out.

John chuckled again. "Why don't you leave us? We're just catching up on old times." John reached to push Luke, but Luke was quicker and pushed him towards the front door.

Just then a group of cops came in. One of them was Wes Tanner, Haley's husband. When John saw the group, he looked back towards her and smiled. "Guess we'll catch up later." His eyes moved to Luke and the smile fell away. Then he turned and left.

She'd been frozen. Her legs were rubbery and she doubted that she would have been able to move even if the building was on fire.

"Are you okay?" Luke stood next to the booth.

She nodded her head, keeping her eyes glued to her hands on the tabletop.

"Hey," he said, sitting across from her, reaching out for her hands. "He didn't hurt you did he?"

She shook her head slowly from side to side. "I'm okay." She focused on her breathing. In. Out. Slowly. Heard each heartbeat as she closed her eyes until her heart settled.

Things came back to her. First, she heard the music pumping from the juke box. Merle Haggard was singing "Mama Tried," a song she'd grown up hearing over and over from her own father's favorite collection.

Then there were the wonderful smells from the kitchen, and she realized she'd come to Mama's not only to work, but to eat.

The fact that John had scared and upset her so much that she'd only thought about running pissed her off.

When her eyes moved up to Luke's, he smiled. "There, that's the look I like to see in those brown eyes of yours." He nodded and leaned back, taking his hand away and crossing his arms over his impressive chest.

"What look?" she asked, taking a deep, cleansing breath.

"The I-should-have-kicked-his-ass look." Her eyebrows shot up. "As opposed to the scared, cornered, kitten from a minute ago."

Her chin rose up quickly. "Scared kitten?"

He laughed and nodded. "If you'd seen yourself a moment ago, you would agree."

Closing her eyes once more, she sighed. "Okay, maybe I can see that. But..." She glanced towards the door, then over to the group of cops sitting across the room, laughing at a joke. "Why I ever wasted a moment dreaming about that boy in school eludes me now."

Luke glanced over towards the door with a slight frown. "Most popular kids grow up to be jerks."

Her eyes moved back towards his. "Didn't you say you used to be popular?"

He smiled. "I suppose so."

"How did you break the stereotype?"

His smile fell away. "That's a long story." He glanced around the brightly lit room. "And one for another time."

She nodded just as a waitress walked up to them.

"Sorry, hun. It's been a zoo in here today. Are ya'll ready to order?"

Luke looked towards her in question, so she nodded quickly. "Join me?" she asked.

His smile was his answer.

They ordered lunch, then talked about some of the terrible things Johnny Drake and his clan had done to her growing up. She even forgot that Christy and Stephany were still sitting across the room from them.

Luke told her stories of what he'd gone through in school. It seemed that even the popular kids had troubles.

She couldn't stop herself from laughing at the story he told of the time he'd been shoved into and locked in the girl's locker room.

"It seemed that the ladies PE teacher had taught them all kickboxing that year." He chuckled and finished off his burger. "I walked out of the locker room ten minutes later with more bruises on me than after football season and basic training combined."

She smiled. "I always thought I was the only one who'd ever gone through something like that."

He leaned forward and pushed his plate to the edge of the table. "So, you've been locked in the lady's locker room before, too?"

She leaned forward. "More than once. However, it was usually after hours and all the lights had been shut off. Or they had stolen all my clothes and I had to wait for my mother to bring me a change of clothes."

His smile slid from his lips. "There's a difference between harmless fun and just being cruel."

"I'm over it." She leaned back and glanced around. The lunch hour had come and gone. Now the place was almost empty and quiet, except for the jukebox wailing out Conway Twitty singing about tight-fitting jeans.

"I..." She swallowed. "I wanted to see if you

wanted to go to the Rusty Rail this Thursday. Alex and Grant are going to try out a few more of my new songs."

"I haven't been there yet."

Her eyebrows shot up, then she smiled. "It's a requirement to live here. I remember the first time my folks took me there. Sunday evenings, they open it up for families. My father used to spin me around the dance floor for hours." She leaned back and lost herself in the memories. "I used to love watching my folks sway on the dance floor. My mother used to be a dancer." She stopped and focused on his eyes. "Ballet." When he nodded, she continued. "She was so smooth. She and my dad were easily the best dancers out on the floor."

"I don't dance," he blurted out. She watched his face and his eyes.

"You don't have to dance, just bring your ears."

He still looked unsure, so she quickly added, "Lauren and Chase are going to be there, too."

"What time?"

"Karaoke starts at five and open mike usually starts around seven."

He nodded, then moved to get out of the booth. He picked up the check and she reached for his hand. "I can—"

He shook his head. "I've got this. Thanks for letting me sit with you. There weren't any open

75

tables when I arrived." He smiled. "I'll see you Thursday."

She nodded and watched him walk to the cashier to pay. She moved back fully into the booth and flipped open her laptop.

The words flew from her fingertips as she typed up a song about her parent's lives that she titled "Smooth Dancers." The story of how they had met had always been one of her favorites. The words on the screen told the story of a dancer falling for a cowboy with two left feet and the years it took them to learn to glide across the dance floor as they fell madly in love with one another.

By the time she shut down her computer, there were tears in her eyes at the beauty she had created and the wonder of her parents' lives.

When she got back to the house, she wrapped her arms around her father and held onto him with everything she had. Here was a man who had grabbed and worked hard for everything he'd ever wanted.

Even though she'd grown up desperately wishing for younger, more hip parents, she realized now that she'd had the best role models she could have ever hoped for. Parents that were not only hardworking, but who actually loved one another, something she'd always dreamed of having one day.

***

Luke shuffled across the floor and wished more than anything that he'd told Tessa he was going to be busy that night. He glanced around the darkened room, searching faces he didn't know as he looked for hers.

Finally, he spotted her near the stage. Walking over to the bar, he ordered a beer to help him relax before making his way towards the front.

"I haven't seen you in here before." If an award could be given for having the sexiest purr, the woman leaning on the bar next to him would have won a medal. The scent of her strong perfume hit him a moment later. Her white shirt was open at the top, showing an impressive amount of cleavage. A large iron cross sat directly between the mounds, causing his eyes to focus on the shiny metal. Her long red hair was tossed over one shoulder and almost matched the color of her lips perfectly. She was wearing a very short pair of shorts and red cowgirl boots.

"First time I've been in here," he said, tossing down some cash for the drink. He turned to make his way towards the front, but the redhead stopped him by putting a hand on his chest and moving closer.

"I'm Christy Hinze." She rubbed her hips up against his. "You're Lucas, right?"

He nodded, feeling all the saliva dry up in his mouth. Okay, so maybe it had been too damn long since he'd enjoyed the feel of a woman next to him. Any woman. Back when he was running around, Christy would have just been what he'd needed.

"Maybe you'd like to join me? I have a private booth"—she tossed her head to the left— "back there. We could be alone, you know, get to know one another."

Her body rubbed up against his and for a moment, he thought about taking her up on the offer, but then the sounds of screaming and tires squealing broke into his mind, almost sending him back a full step. With his empty hand, he set her aside. "Sorry, I'm meeting some friends." He stepped away.

"Maybe next time," she purred in his ear before he walked away.

By the time he reached Tessa and the group she was with, the redhead was already out of his mind and he'd recovered from the sharp memory.

"Wow, I'm impressed," Grant said when he shook his hand. "Most men don't get past Christy the first time."

Luke glanced back at the redhead, who was sitting in her booth with another man she'd pulled into her web. "I've been caught in a web like that before." He turned back to the group.

Grant slapped him on his back. "Some webs are better than others." He walked over and wrapped his arms around his wife.

"You're not the one getting up on the stage, are you?" he asked Tessa.

She turned to him after taking a drink of her own beer. "I will be singing one song." She glanced around the room. "It still makes me nervous. Especially since it's people I know. You'd think that after doing this a few times, it wouldn't bother me so much."

"Few times?" he asked, leaning against the high-top table.

"Sure, we've been trying out my songs here for some time now." She turned and looked around the room again. "There are more people this time than before."

He reached out to run a hand down her arm. "I'm sure everyone will love them."

She chuckled slightly and turned back towards him. "It's stupid, being so nervous."

"No, not at all." His hand once more came up to her skin. She was wearing a black tank top that spilled low in the front and only had a long piece of metal holding it up over each shoulder and down the back. Her jean skirt and black boots were sexier than any heels and dress he'd ever seen on a woman in the city. She had on a black cowgirl hat and large hooped silver earrings, which finished the look perfectly. Her hair was tied back with a black ribbon and curled in loops he wished he could run his fingers through.

He'd denied himself for so long, he was finding it harder and harder to keep his mind off of his desires when he was around her. Funny, he'd had no problem brushing off the redhead a few moments ago, but when it came to Tessa...

He took a deep breath and smelled the soft scent of her perfume and for a moment, dreamed of burying his face in the soft spot behind her ear and drinking it in.

"Maybe if you took a spin around the dance floor first, you might get your mind off of your nerves?"

Her eyes moved to his. "I thought you said you don't dance?"

"Don't. Not can't." He took her hand as the next song started up. He couldn't have planned a better song if he'd tried. Willie Nelson crooned to "Help Me Make It Through the Night."

When he wrapped his arm around her, she moved closer to him and placed her arm over his shoulder and smiled up at him.

"Perfect song," she murmured, and he nodded back.

"That's what I'm here for," he said as he started moving. For the first time in his life, he was grateful for the dance lessons he'd been forced to take as a child in middle school gym class. Thankful that the great state of Texas had always played by their own rules and had kept that requirement for learning.

She felt great in his arms as they moved slowly around the dance floor. Several other couples flooded around them until the small dance floor was completely full.

"This is something I've always dreamed of." She sighed and glanced around.

He smiled. "What? Dancing with me?"

She chuckled and shook her head. "Not that this isn't nice, but this..." She nodded around. "Making people feel this with the words I write. Having couples fall in love while swaying to my songs. Making people think, feel more while listening to something I created."

His smile grew as he moved her closer. "I've always wished I had a talent like you do."

Her eyes moved to his and her eyebrows shot up. "I'm sure there's something you're good at."

He thought about it. "Not really. I mean, in school I was okay at sports. In the forces I was as good as the rest. I've been told I have a good head for business. But, I suck at painting and..." He chuckled at himself. "I couldn't write a poem if my life depended on it. Or, to be more exact, if a relationship depended on it. That's how I lost my very first girlfriend in third grade."

Her chuckle almost caused his steps to falter. The smoothness and sexiness of the soft sound was intoxicating. He was determined to hear it at least a dozen more times that night.

"Well, maybe you have hidden talents..." She moved back slightly and glanced up and down at him. His entire body tightened as her eyes roamed. "You're pretty good at dancing."

"Thank you." He pulled her closer to hide the fact that he was getting a little nervous with her looking at him like that.

"Can you sing?"

He thought about it. "I'm not terrible at it."

"Can you play an instrument?" she asked as the song came to an end.

"I taught myself guitar in high school. My girlfriend..." He shook off the thoughts. "Yeah, I'm okay on guitar."

"I'd like to hear... that is, if you want? Maybe you can help me sometime. I'm mediocre at playing and sometimes I just want to hear what I've written from someone who's better."

He thought about it and nodded as they made their way back to the table. "How about another beer?" He nodded towards her empty glass.

"Sure." She glanced down at her watch and then over to Alex and Grant. "They'll be starting soon."

"I'll be back in a few." He took her empty glass and his and made his way towards the bar.

He had to catch his breath after dancing with

Tessa. Just a moment to catch up on his own thoughts. For his mind to catch up to his body, which was currently full of all sorts of desires. Desires he was trying to avoid at all cost.

"Get bored of Tracy already?" The redhead pushed her entire body up against his.

Moments ago he'd seen her pressing that busty body up against another man as they swayed on the dance floor. Glancing around, he looked for the man, but didn't see him within sight.

"Just getting a few more beers." He nodded to the bartender and held up two fingers. The man nodded and poured two tall ones.

"Well, if you do get bored..." She reached up and slowly slid a piece of paper into his front jean's pocket. Her fingers brushed against him, causing his body to instantly react. He cursed silently and pulled away, then threw a twenty on the counter and grabbed up the two beers and walked away.

By the time he reached Tessa, he was brewing. He hated it when his body reacted and his mind wasn't in control.

"Thanks." She took her beer, biting her bottom lip. He stood by and swallowed half his beer before the end of the next song.

Just then, a woman in her sixties walked up on the stage. The crowd grew quiet and then started yelling and whistling.

"Okay, okay, settle down." She waved her hands and waited out the crowd. "If'n ya'll don't quiet down, you won't be able to hear what we have in store for you tonight."

That settled the crowd down.

"That's better. We've got a great line-up tonight." Several cheers broke out. "First off, I know ya'll have been waiting all week to hear them, Alex and Grant Holton singing Tessa Keys' latest, "Time Will Heal All.""

The crowd erupted as Alex and Grant climbed the stairs to the stage.

He stood back as a soft guitar track started playing over the PA. When Grant started singing, he felt chills travel up his arms, and he had to lean against the table when Alex's voice joined him. It wasn't the music, or the singers, but the words that had his knees growing weak.

The song spoke of time lost, wasted on things that shouldn't matter. It's slow rhythm only added to the sadness of the time passing and the things left and lost behind. By the time the song ended, he felt a soreness in his throat and gut.

He'd felt more in the past three minutes than he'd felt in the seven months since the accident.

He was thankful that Tessa had been occupied joining Alex and Grant on the stage for her song. The couple stood back as Tessa waited for the next track to start.

When her eyes moved over to his, he tried to smile and encourage her, but his emotions were almost out of control.

When Tessa started singing this time it was about beating the Devil at his own game. The rhythm was much faster than the first song, and Tessa's voice was something dreams were made of.

She had a great range and seemed to enjoy standing up on the stage, clapping and getting the crowd into the beat. The lyrics talked about tricking the Devil into thinking she was something instead of nothing. Putting him in his place until finally, she started believing her own lies. Then, when the Devil called on her, he couldn't call the bet, since she had convinced herself she was worth something.

Once again, the song touched him and forced him to think about his own self-worth.

He'd been hiding out in Fairplay for almost a year, with little to nothing to show for it. Sure, he'd closed on his place, fixed a few things here and there, and purchased a head of cattle, all thanks to the very large trust fund from his family's business. He'd moved out to the middle of nowhere to discover himself and get over the pain he'd caused. But instead, he'd just been hiding out. Hiding from himself.

Soon, the room felt too stuffy. There were too many people crowding around him. His ears rang and all he could hear were screams, tires squealing, and the sound of a far-off siren. Even the strobe lights in his eyes were causing his eyes to water. He set his beer down and felt his chest tighten.

His legs moved quickly as he headed towards the back door. He pushed into the night air, hoping for a cool breeze, but instead a quick burst of heat hit him in the chest.

He rushed away from the lights, towards the sound of running water. The full moon overhead helped him see his way. He finally stopped and leaned against a wooden railing. There was a small creek below.

He could hear the crowd going wild inside behind him and wondered how many more songs Tessa had. He knew it was rude of him to be outside while her songs were going, but there were just too many emotions built up in him. He had to get away.

Closing his eyes, he took a couple deep breaths.

He'd never had a women make him feel... so much, before. Sure, he'd loved Lindsay, or so he'd thought, but they hadn't had a relationship. Not really. They'd fallen hard and fast too early. Too young. Then they'd gotten caught up in the tangle of what others had expected from them.

"Hey," her soft voice sounded behind him. "Are you okay?"

He cleared his mind and throat before turning

around and nodding, because he didn't trust his voice.

"I think your songs are a hit." He leaned back against the fence as she walked over and stopped next to him.

"From the sounds of it"—she turned to smile up at him— "I'd say so." She rested her booted foot on the bottom rung and leaned on the fence, closer to him.

The sexy scent of her floated towards him. The look of her face in the moonlight made him wish he could paint. She'd removed her hat before going on stage, and now her hair was floating around her face. She kept pushing it away from her eyes as the warm breeze blew over them.

"I've always loved this time of year." She sighed and glanced over towards the water. "I know most people hate late winter, but it's one of my favorite times of the year."

He turned towards her, his hand going out to brush a strand of dark hair away from her face. "You're an amazing woman," he said softly.

He heard her breath hitch and decided, for the first time in his life, to let his emotions out. He cupped her neck and pulled her a step towards him as he moved closer to her.

"Amazing," he whispered before he touched his heart to hers. Their lips met, softly, slowly, as the moon made its way across the vast dark sky. He took his time, leisurely playing over her soft mouth as his hands roamed over her back, holding her closer to him.

She tasted like heaven and felt like sin. He didn't want to let her go, but when he heard the music die down, he took a slight step back and broke the contact.

"I guess we'd better head back inside." He reached down and took her hand in his and started walking. "I didn't mean to miss that last song," he said, stopping just outside the doors.

"It's okay. Maybe you can swing by later this week and hear it privately," she added before breezing through the door and back into the crowded bar.

Chapter Six

Tessa's knees had gone weak when Luke kissed her last night. Okay, if she was completely honest with herself, everything of hers had gone weak when he'd kissed her. She'd dreamed of him and thought of him every minute since he'd shown up at the bar in his tight worn blue jeans.

Who could blame her? After all, he was the cowboy of every woman's dreams. His thick dark hair was a little too long and had just the right amount of curl to it. His jaw alone could make any woman swoon. When he smiled, he had a slight dimple in his left cheek and a slight dip between his brows when he worried.

There was still so much she wanted to discover about him, but he was so reserved. She had seen pain in his eyes last night when she'd met him outside.

She'd watched him leave from the stage and had worried that he'd hated her songs and just couldn't face her. But something had told her to find out, one way or another. And she was thankful she had.

The old her, Tracy, wouldn't have followed Luke outside. She wouldn't have been kissed under the full moon until she'd felt her toes tingle. But, Tessa…Tessa had.

She couldn't stop the smile as she reached up to hug herself.

Tracy wouldn't have allowed her songs to be published, nor would she have allowed herself to open herself up so much. Even though she knew that ridicule could have been an outcome, she had prepared herself for it. But, so far, no one had said anything negative.

Still, every time she went to the Rusty Rail, she braced and prepared for it. She only wished her mother was still alive to enjoy her music.

She had read her some of her poems the week before she'd passed away. But her mother had been on so many pain meds, she doubted she had heard or understood anything.

"Hey, Daddy," she said, walking into the kitchen and kissing his paper-thin cheek.

Her father was standing at the stove, cooking up

fresh eggs and a pan of bacon.

"Morning." He glanced over at her. She noted the dark circles under his eyes and held back a frown. "How'd it go last night?"

"Wonderful." She gently pushed him aside and finished cooking. "Grab me some OJ, will you?" She knew he'd pour the glass and sit down to read the paper. They had fallen into a pattern the last few weeks. "Luke showed up last night."

"Oh? The boy that helped with the chicken coop?"

She nodded and flipped the bacon over. "He says he plays the guitar and can sing. I was hoping to spend some time with him later this week, working on a few other songs."

"That would be nice, dear." He flipped open his paper.

"What are your plans for the week?"

"Oh, nothing too exciting. I've got to run into town for some more chicken feed and some grain for the animals. I was thinking of mowing the yard later this week."

She set the spatula down and turned towards him, her hands on her hips. "We talked about this."

He glanced up at her. "Now, Theresa..." He only used her full name when he was trying to assert his authority.

"Don't Theresa me, Dad. You're too fragile to

91

be pulling around that old mower. Besides, I could use the exercise." She turned back towards the pan of bacon. "Especially since you keep feeding me bacon."

"I don't want to become a burden. You know, I've been thinking of selling this ol' place."

She dropped the spatula into the eggs and spun around. "What?"

"Sure. I mean, I'm not as young as I was when we bought this place." He sighed and glanced out the window. "I built that chicken coop, myself. Reroofed the house and the barn myself, too." He turned to her and she could see tears in his eyes.

"What's brought this on?" She flipped off the burners and walked over to sit next to him and took his hand in hers.

"Your mother's funeral took a lot of out me, and our savings." He glanced down at their joined hands. "We hadn't planned. You know, you watch those commercials that tell you to plan ahead. Well, we kept denying that either one of us was going to die. Then, well, Leslie got sick and... then we were paying medical bills and then funeral bills."

"Dad, I'm here. Let me help."

"Why? What for? This ol' place?" He shook his head. "No, I've sunk enough money into this place over the years. Truth was, I only fixed the chicken coop roof so the place could sell better."

"Oh, Dad." She felt her heart slip a little, thinking about some other family living in her house, the only family home she'd ever known. "We'll figure something out." She patted his hand. "First, let's eat."

Three mornings later, she stood outside of Mama's and sighed. "This is only temporary," she told herself. A few shifts here and there. Just until she made a few more checks on her songs.

"You ready?" Mama asked when she walked through the door.

"I suppose so." She wiped her sweaty hands on her skirt. "Show me the ropes."

Two hours later, she had the swing of things. Why had she figured it would be so hard? Maybe because every time she was in the place, it was packed. Glancing around now, there were only four people sitting at tables.

She supposed during rush hour things would get a little more complicated, but for now, she was happy to start the early shift. She'd arrived shortly after the breakfast rush, which had helped. When she glanced down at her watch, she figured she had another half an hour before the lunch rush would hit.

She glanced over the menu once more, even though she knew the darn thing frontwards and backwards, since she'd eaten there all of her life and the menu hadn't changed once. Well, they were now printed on fancier stock paper coated in plastic, as opposed to the old paper place mats Mama used to have.

She also took the time to make sure she knew how to ring up everything in the computer system.

"It's a lot easier now dat I got dis"—Mama patted the computer screen— "after dat twister took out my ol' one." A thick rich chuckle vibrated from her ample chest. "I fig'rd I was due an upgrade."

"It does seem to help." She had rung in the last four orders with ease.

"Why don't you grab somethin' to eat before da rush comes." She patted her arm. "Just tell ol' Willard what you want."

Willard, one of the longtime cooks at Mama's, was one of the nicest men in town. Tessa could remember coming in to the diner, feeling down after having problems at school, and Willard would be there with a large chocolate shake.

"Thanks." She walked towards the back kitchen area.

Willard was at his usual place behind the grill. When he noticed her, he turned towards her with a smile.

"So? What'd I tell you?"

"Thanks." She walked over to him and wrapped her arms around him. "For the job and for the

94

advice."

He chuckled and patted her arm. "Ol' Willard would never steer you wrong."

She'd run into the man two days ago at the Grocery Stop. They had talked about her father's financial problems and Willard had suggested she work part time at Mama's, since they were shorthanded. All three of the West sisters had once waitressed at Mama's when they had been desperately trying to keep their family farm. She figured, if it was good enough for them, then it was good enough for her.

"I made your favorite." He nodded to a plate sitting on the countertop. "The milk shake is in the freezer." He winked, then turned back to his work.

"You make this job totally worth it," she said after biting into her burger.

By the time she walked out front again, the place was starting to pack out. Near the end of her shift, she wondered if she'd made the right choice. Her feet were throbbing, her lower back hurt, and she was pretty sure she was going to have nightmares of numbers and the computer screen freezing again, all night long.

As she walked back to her car, rubbing her lower back, she wondered how much she was willing to do to keep her father in the large place.

He'd tried to convince her that he'd be much happier in a smaller place in town. A place where he didn't have to do all the yardwork.

Still, she was determined to keep her childhood home. But she'd figured out exactly what it was going to take to keep it, and it wouldn't be easy. Her folks had taken out a second mortgage to help pay for some of the medical bills, which meant almost double the payments. There were other loans as well, two of them, totaling several thousand dollars.

Honestly, she didn't know how she was going to be able to afford paying those off and keep making the mortgage payments. Not to mention, feeding her father and paying off her own school bills.

As she drove out of town, she noticed the 'For Rent' sign on Savannah and Billy's old place and remembered Savannah offering up the place to her, if she wanted.

Swinging her car around, she headed to where she knew Savannah would be— Holly's Coffee & Wine Bar. It was just down the street from Mama's. Savannah ran the kids' corner after-school program.

When she walked in, April, the longtime employee, greeted her.

"There's our famous writer now." She smiled. Tessa noted the woman's standard streak of pink in her hair.

"How's it going? Have those kids of yours

broken any hearts lately?"

April chuckled. "You know it."

"Is Savannah around?" She glanced towards the back area.

"She should be done with reading hour soon." April glanced down at her watch. "How about a drink to tide you over?"

She was about to turn the woman down, but then thought about her swollen feet and decided she would really enjoy getting off them for a while. Walking over, she sat down at the bar.

"What'll you have?"

"Something sweet and strong."

"Sounds like you had a hard first day at Mamas."

"No, I suppose it's just a normal day. I don't know how people do it. Standing on their feet for so long."

"Shift."

"Hmm?" She waited until April set a light pink drink with floating berries in front of her.

"Shift from one leg to another. The key is movement." She showed her by swaying from one leg to another slightly. "It helps your feet and your back."

Just then, a very loud group of kids came rushing past them, followed slowly by their parents.

Tessa waited until all of them were gone before walking towards the back. Savannah was kneeling down, picking up several books from the floor.

"Hey." She walked over and helped.

"Oh." She glanced over, then frowned. "So, it's true. You are working at Mama's?"

"Yup, started today."

She stood up and set the books on the table. "So, you are staying?"

"I… I still haven't decided."

"Augh!" Savannah growled out, then glanced over to where her two kids were still playing quietly. "Why can't you just make up your mind and stick around? I mean, aren't you happy here?"

"For now." She wasn't technically happy, but she didn't want to go into it with Savannah just now.

"Well, then commit." She tossed the books into her bag. "Besides, what would you do without your friends around?" She turned back towards her and smiled. "What would we do without you here? For the few years you were gone, we all suffered?"

Tessa couldn't hold in the laughter. "You really are a drama queen."

"No, I used to be a drama queen. Now, I'm a drama goddess." She crossed her arms over her chest and laughed.

"Okay, I'll commit to staying around until we sell our house."

"What?" Savannah stood back up and moved towards her. "So you and your father are really moving out of Fairplay?"

"No, actually, I was hoping you might be able to help us out. Dad needs a place to stay. A place that is hopefully cheaper than paying two mortgages."

"What about you?"

She bit her lip. "That place of yours was pretty small."

"One of the reasons we moved out when I was pregnant with Audrey. Maggie's room was only big enough for one toddler."

She sighed. "But, the place would be perfect for dad."

"What about upstairs?" Savannah added.

"I didn't know there was an upstairs to that place."

"No, not that place. This one." She pointed upwards with her fingers.

"I'm not following you." She glanced up with a frown.

"Holly's old apartment upstairs. It has its own private entrance and I'm sure Holly and Travis will rent it out to you really cheap, since it's been empty for the last year. Besides, you're practically family." She wrapped her arm around her. "If you want, April has the keys. You can go on up and take a look at it."

"I… I'm not sure. I hadn't planned on replacing two mortgage payments with rent on two places."

"Well, we were charging six hundred for our place, but I think we can go as low as four-fifty."

Tessa almost choked on thin air. "What? That low? How can you afford—"

"Honey, the place is paid off. We just charge for upkeep. Another thing your dad won't have to worry about. We have a guy that does all the yard work and fixes anything that needs to be done."

"Wow." She did some calculations in her head. "How much does Holly's place go for?"

"You'll have to talk to her. But it's only a one room place, so I would think right around the same as we charge. Call her and ask." She walked over and took her bag. "Kids, we have to go make dinner for daddy."

The kids jumped up and rushed towards her. After briefly saying hi and answering some of the standard kid questions that flew from Savannah's kids at a rapid pace, she walked towards the front with them.

"Your dad can move in anytime. Just let me know and I'll get the keys to you."

"Thanks." She almost walked out with her, but Savannah stopped her. "April, give Tessa the keys to upstairs. She wants to look the place over."

"Will do. By sweeties." She waved to the kids. "See you tomorrow."

"Night." Savannah turned back towards her. "Think about it." She moved to go, but stopped. "And stay in town." She winked and left.

"Here they are," April said after a moment. "The entrance is out back. Just up the stairs."

"Thanks." She took the key ring and walked towards the door. It was funny, her car was parked right by the stairs, and she'd never known the apartment was up there. Glancing up, she thought of how nice it would be to live in town.

Her dorm room had been on campus, and there hadn't been anything close. It had been at least a five-minute drive to the nearest coffee shop. Now, she was thinking of living above one.

Still, just the thought of paying two rents made her head ache. Maybe she should look for a different home in town, one big enough for both her and her father?

When the door slid open, she instantly knew she wanted the place. Large windows overlooked the main street of Fairplay. There was a beautifully remodeled kitchen near the back of the building. She walked into the bedroom and liked the size and the large windows that overlooked the side of the building. When she walked into the bathroom, she gasped and fell in love with the place.

There was a large garden bathtub, which sat next to a huge glass-walled shower with stone tiles. Double sinks sat on a marble countertop that ran on the inside wall. The large frosted window, which she assumed overlooked the back alley, let in natural light and made it look cheery.

There were dark oak floors and the walls were painted a soft gray with crisp white crown molding. The kitchen cabinets were off-white French Country style. She'd never seen anything more beautiful before.

She took her time walking around the place, looking out the large windows and enjoying setting up everything in her mind. She'd never had a space of her very own before. She'd also never had a man kiss her the way Luke had the other night. Nor had she ever felt the way she did when she was around him.

Her mind kept telling to get out of Fairplay as quickly as possible, but her heart... She was worried about her father and excited about the possibilities with Luke.

By the time she walked the key back downstairs, she was determined to make the finances work and even more determined to stay in Fairplay until Luke kissed her again.

Chapter Seven

*W*hy did it seem that everything working against him? He'd been planning on painting his deck and working in the yard, but glancing out the window, he frowned at the rain streaming down at an alarming rate.

The south was known for its torrential rains, but this was just plan ridiculous. He'd been locked in his house for almost three full days. His backyard and parts of his driveway were now under so water, he was thinking of renting a backhoe and having several loads of dirt delivered, just to smooth his yard out so the water didn't stick too long in several areas. He even spent some time drawing his yard and trying to figure out how to get the rain water to flow towards the back of his property where there was a creek running away from his land.

Nothing could be worse than spending three days alone in a house with nothing to do. Being not only physically but mentally locked away was making him wonder why he'd decided to move into the middle of nowhere.

At first he'd done everything in his power to keep mentally busy. But, after a while, he'd found himself drifting deep into the back of his mind, even if he didn't want to.

The worse day of his life played over and over in his mind. He'd driven into town and spent as much time as he could, walking around the big hardware store, but after bumping into too many people who all had too many questions about his past, he was done trying to wait his boredom out.

But what had really sealed the deal with him was when he'd run into Christy at the Grocery Stop. The woman just couldn't take a hint, and he was finding it almost appalling how she flung herself at him. It made him wonder just how many men in town actually fell for her act.

So, he'd decided he wouldn't spend any more time around town, hoping he'd run into Tessa. He buckled down and stayed at home.

Instead of being bored, he embraced being alone by pulling out his guitar and spending time tuning it. Then he spent the next day and a half playing every song he could remember. He even worked on one of Tessa's songs from last week.

He'd thought about calling her, but every time he did, he remembered how raw he'd felt after hearing her sing. The truth was, he didn't think he was ready for that kind of emotion. The emotions and her.

He'd been at a different place in his life last year, before he'd started dating Kristen again. He'd had several other girlfriends over the years, and even in basics, after he'd haltingly proposed to her, he'd run around on her.

He'd never really felt guilty about being with other women during that time. Maybe it was because he knew he'd made a big mistake asking Kristen to marry him. After all, all through school, they'd broken up and gotten back together so many times, he'd lost count.

After school, things had changed and he knew everyone, including his parents, had all but planned out their wedding. But if the military had taught him one thing, it was that he no longer wanted to just fall in line with what other's wanted for his life.

That's why he was here, in the middle of Texas, alone, without telling anyone where he'd disappeared to. He'd needed to escape the memories and guilt, but more important, he'd needed to escape the look everyone gave him. The look that said, "Oh, your heart is broken and you're the one to blame."

He'd had enough of it. Enough of everyone telling him what he should or shouldn't do with his life. So, he'd done the first thing that had come to his mind. He'd cashed out a few stocks his father had given him as a graduation gift and run.

He'd stopped in Fairplay on a whim and noticed the property auction sign. It had either been fate or sheer dumb luck that he'd had just enough to purchase the place. He'd pulled every last dime from his checking account to fix the place up and was surviving on his savings account. He still wasn't sure what he was going to do for the rest of his life, but so far he was content planning out his cattle and learning how to be a full-time rancher.

He knew that he always had the option of crawling home, where there were even more stock options and trust funds—and all his troubles—but he was determined to stick it out. Even if it meant spending several days locked in his mind alone, waiting out the rain.

When the sun finally did show again, he'd worked out a lot of things. First and foremost, he wasn't ready for a relationship again, but was very interested in playing guitar some more. He'd even thought about showing up to the Rusty Rail next Thursday night to sit up on the stage himself.

He'd forgotten how much playing music made him forget things. To him, music was the best medicine. The more he played and sang, the more he felt healed and, after what he'd been through, he was determined to feel that way as often as he could.

With his guitar in the back seat of his truck, he headed towards Tessa's place. He was shocked to see a 'For Sale' sign out front with the red sticker across it marked Sold.

She hadn't told him that her father was thinking of selling the place. Then again, he hadn't really opened up to her, so how could he expect her to open up to him?

He parked his truck and realized her car wasn't in the driveway. He'd been about to back out, but then noticed her father sitting on the front porch and stepped out to greet the older man.

"Hi," he called out.

"Evening." He continued to swing. "Theresa's at work right now."

"Work?" he asked as he stepped up onto the front porch.

The man nodded. "She started last week at Mama's." Luke frowned and stopped at the top step. "She's already moved into her new place in town. I'm moving into my new place this weekend. The new owners are supposed to be here on Monday. I can't believe how fast it all happened." He sighed and glanced around the front yard. "I'm going to miss this place." Then he smiled. "I'm not going to miss the upkeep though."

Luke glanced around and nodded. "It is a pretty big place." He shoved his hands deep into his jean pockets. "Where is Tessa's new place?"

"Above Holly's place."

"And yours?"

"The little blue house right down the street. She made a deal with Savannah and Billy Jackson. Got me a good deal on rent there." He stopped swinging. "Never thought I'd want to live in town again, but..." He started to swing again. "At my age, I need to be close to people again."

He wasn't sure what to say, so he remained silent for a while.

"Leslie and I always planned on watching our grandkids running around this old place, but we waited so long to have kids ourselves that we ran out of time. When you're young, you always think you have more time than you do. We were in our late forties when we had Theresa. She had a hard time growing up, because we were older. We could hardly keep up with her." He chuckled. "My god that child could go. She was running from the time she could walk. It seemed we were always trying to catch up with her." The man's eyes floated off towards the yard and Luke could see that he was lost in a memory. "We were too selfish when we were young. We wanted to travel, see places, experience things before we settled down to a family." He sighed and his eyes grew sad. "You know the funny thing was, with all our travels and excitement, it's the times with our daughter that we cherished the most." He turned back towards Luke. "Don't wait too long to grab happiness." He shook his head slightly. "I don' meant to preach at ya, but…"

Luke nodded. "I understand." He leaned against the post. "My folks were barley twenty when they had me. It didn't stop them from doing what they wanted, going where they wanted. My dad took over my grandfather's business when I was fifteen. That's when they had to settle down."

He nodded in agreement. "We should have given Theresa a brother or sister, but Leslie… well, we were lucky to have one." His eyes moved back to his. "You want kids?"

He almost coughed, but cleared his throat instead. "I hadn't given it much thought." It was a lie, but he couldn't bring himself to say it out loud. At least not yet.

"Some advice from an old man… find an answer. Sooner rather than later." He stood up and rolled his shoulders and stretched. "And do it soon enough so you can enjoy grandkids." He walked to the front door. "Tessa gets off at eight." He smiled and winked then walked inside.

***

She was made for this kind of work. It had been

almost a week since she'd started at Mama's. To say she'd gotten the hang of it would be an understatement. Working a job like this gave her plenty of time to dream about her music. The people that came and went gave her other things to write about.

She imagined the stories of the couples that came in and snuggled in the back booths. Then she wrote those stories down. She imagined the friends that laughed and joked with one another, the older people's lives and stories.

Since starting at Mama's, she'd written over a dozen new songs. Never had she been more inspired. Not even when she'd been so emotional herself.

Of course, she'd written a song about Lucas and the kiss. Which she had no intention of ever letting him see. Or anyone else for that matter.

Her shift was over in less than half an hour. She planned to finish unpacking her place and then spend some time on her laptop, buying a few more things online.

When the bell chimed, she glanced over to greet the customers, and her smile grew when she saw Luke walk in.

"Hi. Sit wherever you want. I'll be with you in a minute."

He nodded and took an empty booth. She delivered the tray of food and then took a moment to straighten her blouse before walking over to his table.

"When did you start working here?" he asked, glancing over his menu.

"Last Thursday." She didn't know why, but she was nervous about him finding out about her job. She knew people now believed she was staying in town, but the truth was, she didn't know herself if she was going to stay or go. She was thankful that Holly and Travis were letting her rent the apartment month to month.

Her father had signed a year lease with Savannah and Billy. She figured, after a year, if he was happy there, they would sign a longer lease.

"You look happy enough." He set his menu down and smiled up at her and she felt her heart skip. The dimple on the side of his mouth was almost too sexy.

"I am." She tilted her head slightly as her eyes ran over him. "You look like you have a secret." She crossed her arms over her chest and waited as his eyebrows shot up.

"Secret? No, but I did bring my guitar to your house, only to find out that you'd moved." He tilted his head and looked at her, much like she'd done to him. "Sounds like you're the one with the secrets."

She held in a chuckle. "I moved above Holly's. My dad moves in to Savannah and Billy's old place across the street this weekend." She glanced over as someone, two tables down, called her. "I'll be right back to take your order."

"I'll be here. You get off in half an hour?" She nodded. "Join me after?"

She smiled at him, giving him his answer with a quick nod.

When she finally put his order in, she added an extra burger in for herself. When the order was up, she closed out of her station and delivered their food and sat across from him.

"It's amazing how great it feels to get off your feet." She tucked her feet under her as she opened her napkin.

"I remember basic training when they had us running most of the day." He poured some ketchup on his plate. "I had bruises on my heels."

"That's why I wear these shoes. I bought the memory foam kind." She sighed. "Saved my feet."

He chuckled. "Don't you love technology?"

"So," she said after taking a bite of her burger, "you brought your guitar?"

His dark eyes moved up to hers. "I've been locked in the house for three days. So, I pulled out the guitar out and tuned it."

"Do you know many songs?" She grabbed a French fry from his plate. She regretted not ordering some for herself, but figured she could

112

get away with snagging a few more of his, since she had planned on sharing some of Willard's chocolate cream pie with him.

"I taught myself every song I could find online." He finished off his ice tea, so she got up and grabbed him some more.

"I took several classes." She frowned. "Okay, so I flunked several classes before I finally got the gist of it." She chuckled. "It seems I have no talent for finding a rhythm."

"I've heard you sing. That's not true."

She smiled. "You've heard the polished Tessa. You should have heard me a few years back." She laughed at the memory. "One of my teachers in college was pretty sure I had what he called opposite rhythm."

"Opposite?"

"If there is such a thing, he was pretty sure I had it." She sighed. "He was one of the most patient men I knew. He's the reason I turned my poems into songs. That day, things with the guitar just… clicked. I suppose it was because I had a reason to play. Something to play to."

She could see in his eyes that he understood. She'd never talked about her struggles to anyone before. It felt wonderful and scary at the same time. Especially, since it was Luke she was opening up to.

"Would you like some pie?" she asked when he

113

took the last bite of his burger. "Willard makes the best chocolate cream pie... My treat."

"I never turn down pie." He smiled and pushed his plate away.

"I'll be right back." She rushed from the table, carrying their empty plates.

"Honey, you better grab that one," Carol, one of the other waitresses, said as she entered the back kitchen. "That boy is something to look at." She sighed as she headed back out front with a tray full of food.

"I'm trying," she thought as she cut an extra-large piece of pie and put a scoop of vanilla ice cream on the side.

Sharing a piece of pie and ice cream was even more romantic than she'd ever imagined. Luke was such a gentleman. He even gave her the last bite. He watched her lips as she licked the sweet cream from them.

She'd spent years imagining a scene like this before, but her imagination paled in comparison to reality.

By the time they walked out the front door, her entire body was aware that he was standing beside her.

"If you want, you're welcome to come up to my place?" She felt her face heat when his eyebrows shot up. "To play... guitar." She almost choked it out. "That was the reason you came into town?"

She closed her eyes and took a deep breath as he chuckled at her.

"If you're sure you're not too tired? I'd like to bring my guitar over."

She opened her eyes and saw his dark ones laughing back at her, but there was more kindness there than humor. Not trusting her voice, she dipped her head and started walking. He put his hand in hers and pulled her to a stop. "Let me grab my guitar." He nodded over towards his truck.

"Oh, sure." She followed him to his truck and watched his backside as he reached in to get his guitar. Her mouth watered when his jeans stretched over his butt. They were worn and bleached, and fit him perfectly. She ached to get her hands on him and wondered if he felt as good as he looked.

When he turned around, her eyes were still lowered and she found herself salivating once more at his front package. Her imagination ran full force, until he coughed. Her face heated once more, and her eyes jumped to his face before she turned around and started walking towards her place.

"I like living in town," she blurted out. "I can walk to work, the grocery store…" She continued to chatter all the way back to her place. By the time they reached the staircase, she was pretty sure he'd gotten over catching her staring at the sexy bulge in his jeans.

115

As she reached to unlock her front door, he set his guitar case down, took her shoulders in his hands, and turned her around to face him.

"I think we'd better get this out of the way, first." He pulled her closer until his breath fell on her face. She could smell his shampoo and aftershave and the mixture of the scents drove her crazy. Then her eyes moved to his and she realized he was watching her mouth once more.

When his head finally dipped down, and their lips touched, she felt her insides liquefy.

Chapter Eight

He knew it was going to happen, sooner or later. He'd thought he was prepared, after the first kiss, but he was wrong.

She was softer than he remembered. Her taste on his lips was sweeter. The soft moan of pleasure that escaped her was sexier. Nothing could have prepared him for her. Nothing.

If he didn't make a conscious effort to pull back, he'd end up... well, he didn't want to think about what he wanted to do to her.

So, he took a big step backwards and almost tripped over his guitar case. "Um." He held in a laugh. "Um," he said again and was thankful when she turned around and opened the door.

"Come on in. I'm still unpacking, so it's kind of a mess." He could hear the nerves in her voice and searched his mind for some way to remove them.

There were a handful of boxes on the floor with half their contents spilled out. The apartment was big and open. He estimated that the living room alone was around eight-hundred square feet and he was surprised at how big the place was.

She had an old sofa he was sure he had seen in her father's house tucked against one of the walls in the living room. He assumed her bedroom sat near the back.

The kitchen was bigger than he'd imagined would fit into a place this size. It was all new equipment and very high tech compared to his own kitchen, which gave him several ideas on how to remodel the space.

"I like the place." He turned around as he set his guitar next to the sofa. "What made you decide to sell your dad's house and move here?"

"My father," she said as she walked towards the kitchen. "I think he saw me struggling to fix up the place…" She held up a beer for him. When he nodded, she flipped the top open with her belt buckle and handed it to him.

At that moment, he was more impressed with her than he'd ever been with another woman in his entire life. His eyes were glued to her as she walked around, a cheap beer in her hand as she looked out the large windows, talking about how her father had struggled financially since her mother passed. He hung on every word until she turned around and frowned over at him.

"Is there a problem with the beer?" She glanced down at the cold bottle in his hand that he'd all but forgotten. He'd been too mesmerized by watching her. She'd untied her hair from a long braid and had been finger combing it while she looked at the dying sunlight outside her window.

The sunlight caught her hair, making it glow and even though he wasn't one for spouting poems or writing songs, a million words flooded his mind. If he had to, he could describe exactly how she looked at that moment and more important, what it did to him to watch her.

"No, it's good," he answered her after swallowing a long drink. The cold liquid did little to cool off his insides, but he took a few more drinks before setting it down. When he picked up his guitar case, she moved to the wall that held her guitar, then stopped and glanced down.

"Would you mind if I got out of my uniform?"

Instantly, images of her in nothing but a sexy pair of panties and a matching bra flashed through his mind. She must have guessed, because she blushed. Her eyes turned soft and she bit her bottom lip, a move that was both sexy and inviting.

"I mean... I smell like burger grease. I'll just...

be a minute." She rushed towards the back and disappeared into what he assumed was the bathroom.

He pulled out his guitar and spent the next few minutes tuning it. He noticed some sheet music she'd written on sitting on the table and decided to give it a try.

By the time she walked back out, he'd gotten the hang of the song. He was singing along softly to the words on the paper and didn't notice her standing in the doorway watching him until he stopped playing.

"I like this one." He waited, but when she didn't say anything, he started getting worried. "What? I didn't think my playing was that bad." He shifted the guitar on his lap.

"No!" She took a step forward. "You have a great… everything." She blushed again. "I… I hadn't planned on showing that song to anyone." She blushed even more.

"Why?" He glanced down at the paper. "It's wonderful."

"It's just…" She edged forward, then stopped and looked down at the paper. "Nothing. What about this one?" She tried to put another song over that one, but he stopped her.

"Actually, I'd like to keep working on this one. I was kind of thinking… Maybe I can play it next Thursday?"

"Next Thursday?" She shifted. "You? This… song?"

"Tessa, is there something wrong with this song?" He set his guitar down and reached for the paper, but she stopped him.

"No!" She closed her eyes as she took a couple deep breaths. "It's just…"

"It's about me?" He tried to hide the smile, but lost the battle. When her eyes flew open and zeroed in on him, the smile grew.

"How…" Her mouth looked so good as it made the sexy oval.

"It's not hard." He took her hand. "I'm not only very flattered, but very turned on." He tugged lightly on her hand until she was sprawled next to him. "I've never had someone write me a song before." He loved the feeling of her soft body pressed against his. She didn't smell like greasy burgers, but sexy flowers and the spring air. He wanted to bury his face in her dark hair and breathe it in, but her skin called to him first.

When his lips brushed over the tender spot under her chin, he felt her shift towards him. Her hips pushed against his, making him wish his worn jeans were a little looser.

His hands roamed over her hips as his mouth took a tour of her soft skin. Her fingers gripped his hair, holding him to her, guiding him where she wanted.

121

When his mouth finally covered hers, he'd pulled her onto his lap. Her legs straddled his hips, causing his jeans to grow even tighter.

His fingers dug into her soft hips as they moved slowly over him, and for the first time in almost a year, he was willing to let his body veto his mind.

***

Tessa's fingers shook as she held Luke's lips to hers. His fingers brushed up her hips, under her T-shirt, until his warm hands played over her sides, causing her to let out a soft chuckle when he brushed her ticklish spot.

She pulled back slightly. She wanted nothing more than to pull every last piece of clothing off him, but she wasn't sure she was ready and that weighed heavily on her.

Ready for him, for sex, for everything. She could tell that he wanted her. It was apparent. She'd been rubbing herself up against him and knew what it meant.

It wasn't that she didn't want to have sex with him, but she needed more... first.

"Sorry, I guess I'm ticklish there."

He smiled up at her and she wondered how she was going to fight the desire to rip all of his clothes off him when he looked at her like that.

"Maybe we can go over a couple other songs before you make a decision on the song..." She started to move aside, but his hands on her hips stopped her. "I'm not…" She closed her eyes, unsure of what to say.

"I understand." He sighed and pulled her close. When she felt his warm breath on her neck, she melted into his arms. "Let's work on this one." He nudged her back until she met his eyes. "I really like it and think it has a chance of becoming something big."

"Really?" She stopped herself from biting her lip again.

"Sure." His hands spanned her hips and set her back on the sofa next to him. "Here, listen." He picked up his guitar and started playing it. She was surprised that he didn't even have to glance down at the music or the lyrics she'd written. Instead, his eyes were glued to hers as he sang her song back to her in one of the sexiest voices she'd ever heard.

By the time he'd finished, she was pretty sure she could claw off his clothes and drag him into her bedroom and enjoy every last minute of it without feeling guilty.

"Well?" He shifted his guitar.

She shook her head slightly. "I… I'm speechless."

"In a good way?" She thought he added, "I hope," under his breath.

She nodded her head several times as she swallowed all the emotions that had welled up.

Just hearing his voice mixed with her words about his kiss and what it had done to her made her believe that he'd felt the same way, but she didn't want to assume.

"I think you're going to be the next big thing at the Rusty Rail." She smiled. "Might even be the best thing to ever happen to the Rusty Rail," she joked. Humor was an easy mask and laughter helped cover the loud beating of her heart.

"Can I take this?" He picked up the sheet of music.

"Um..." She started to think of a reason, an excuse.

"Tessa." He set his guitar down, and reached for her hand. "If I'm going to sing this in a few nights, I'd like to make sure I know it by heart."

She sighed and then, a moment later, nodded.

"Good. I'd like to take a couple more." He reached over and showed her the four songs she'd finished that week. "If it's okay with you?"

She closed her eyes, trying to hide the fear. "Sure."

His chuckle caused her eyes to fly open. "Don't worry, everyone's going to love them. I figured we'd do this one together." He set a sheet on top. He nodded towards her guitar. "Of course, we'd have to spend some time practicing together."

On rubbery legs, she walked over and pulled

down her guitar. When they started playing together, it was like magic.

He started singing the part she'd marked for Grant, and she started singing Alexis' part.

It was strange to have her voice pitched perfectly with his. She'd never sung with a partner before. She'd always assumed it took a lot of practice. Alex and Grant had made it look easy and now she knew it was.

Their voices wove in and out from one another and matched perfectly as the last chord played out.

The room was silent at the end and she felt a tear slide down her cheek.

"That's a powerful one."

She swallowed. "It was for my parents."

"I'm sure your mother would have loved it."

He put his guitar back in its case and tucked the papers on top of it. "I think we've got that one down. Don't you?" He glanced over his shoulder at her.

"Yes, I'd say so."

"What time do you get off tomorrow?"

"Eight." She stood up and hung her guitar back up.

"I'm going to have to get a couple of those hooks." When she turned around, he was right behind her and she almost bumped into him.

"Hum?"

"The hooks you have." He nodded to the wall where four guitars hung, all with different colored lights shining on them from the ceiling.

"Oh, they have them online." She smiled. "I'm kind of a freaky online shopper."

He chuckled. "Well, maybe you can forward me the link." His hands went to her hips and he pulled her closer. "Of course, I only have the one guitar."

Her eyebrows shot up. "The way you play, you should have a few. I can let you borrow my electric one here." She stepped away and took her prized guitar down from the wall.

"This is a custom Martin!" He turned it over in his hands, feeling the weight of it, and then sat on the sofa and strummed it. It was a custom black job she'd found at a pawn shop in Austin. She'd immediately maxed out her credit cards to get it. But she had to admit, it looked and sounded better with him than it ever had with her.

"I can't take this—"

"Take it. You'll want to practice on it before next week." She walked to her closet and pulled out its hard case and the small amp that went with it. "Have you ever played on an electric?"

He nodded, his eyes still glued to the guitar. "I'll borrow this on one condition." She waited. "If you let me help move your dad this weekend."

126

She laughed. "It's a deal." She held out her hand and, instead of shaking it, he set the guitar down and pulled her into his arms.

"And, if we continue this…" His lips brushed hers. When he pulled back, she smiled.

"It's a deal."

Chapter Nine

The next few days went by quickly. Every night Luke showed up at the diner. They ate dinner, then walked down to her place for practice. Every night he kissed her until they were both breathless. Then he would pack up and head home.

That weekend, along with half a dozen others, he helped move her dad into the small house on Main Street.

By Sunday evening, he was settled in and she could tell he was much happier.

When she walked to work on Monday, she stopped by and saw him sitting out front on the porch talking to the neighbor, Mrs. Cole. The woman was old, but looked younger than her father.

She stopped dead in her tracks when she saw Mrs. Cole fluff her fair as she talked to her father.

She was going to laugh it off as harmless old-people flirting until she saw her father pat the woman's hand.

"Hey, Dad," she burst in, causing them both to jump slightly. She figured he deserved the scare.

"Oh." He chuckled. "I guess we were too busy gossiping to see you walk up."

"Yeah." She stretched out the word as her eyes moved over to Mrs. Cole.

"You remember Martha Cole," her father said, making sure his hand was tucked into his jeans.

"Sure, you taught me in third grade." She smiled at the woman. She had nothing but fond memories of the woman. But that didn't mean she wanted her sniffing around her dad.

"Heading to work, sweetie?" he asked.

"Yes, I wanted to stop by and see if you needed anything from the store. I have to stop by on the way back."

"Nope, I walked over there this morning when they opened their doors. I was out of eggs."

"Oh," Mrs. Cole broke in. "You should have come on over. I made a whole pan of eggs and bacon this morning." She turned towards Tessa. "I just can't seem to cook for one." She sighed. "Ever since my Harold died, I still cook enough food for two." Mrs. Cole winked at Tessa, which, somehow, made Tessa feel more at ease.

"I couldn't intrude…" her father said.

"Oh shush, it's no intrusion. After all, we're neighbors now." She reached over and patted his hand.

"Well," Tessa broke in, "if you don't need anything." She felt an almost urgent need to get out of there. "Oh." She snapped her fingers and turned back towards them. "Dad, I was wondering if you wanted to come listen to Luke sing some of my songs at the Rusty Rail this Thursday."

"Oh!" Mrs. Cole smiled. "How exciting."

"Well, I suppose." Her father turned to Mrs. Cole. "I'd love to go. That is, if you'd care to join me?"

She tried not to grind her teeth as she walked away as they made their plans. For the rest of the day, she was in a mood. Work didn't hold its charm like it had. When Lucas showed up at a quarter to eight, she had a full-blown headache and tried to call off their practice for the night.

But sitting across from him eating fried catfish, she couldn't bring herself to turn him away. Besides, maybe a good old-fashioned make-out session would do her mood some good.

When she opened her door, she didn't even give him a chance to set the guitar case down before her lips were on his. She pushed him back against the

131

front door, slamming it behind him. The guitar case hit the carpet as she pushed his shirt open, and reached to pull his T-shirt from his jeans.

She was right, kissing him made all the other thoughts go away. Instead, her mind was on how to get him naked. What it would feel like to lay next to him. Skin to skin.

She tugged his shirt over his head, then ran her fingers over his impressive chest. It was smooth and rock hard. His muscles jumped under her fingers as she played over them. She dipped her head and ran her tongue over his pecs, something she'd always dreamed of trying. His fingers dug into her hair as her fingers explored lower to play with the buttons on his jeans.

Before she could open them, he reached down and took her wrists with his hands, then reversed their positions until her back was up against the wood of her door.

He pushed her shirt open, exposing her skin, causing goosebumps to rise all over as his hands and mouth roamed over her. She closed her eyes tight and enjoyed the feeling of his warm mouth on her. When one of his fingers pushed aside her bra, her breath hitched. The tip of his finger circled her nipple, causing it to pucker for him, then he dipped his head and replaced his finger with the tip of his tongue.

She'd never experienced anything more exciting in her entire life. She questioned if she was ready for everything that came with intimacy, but when his mouth moved back up to hers, all the doubts flew away.

Her breath was labored when he pulled back and ran his eyes over her.

"What brought this on?" He sounded winded.

"Does a woman need a reason to rip a man's clothes off?" She ran her eyes over his half-naked body, enjoying the look of him.

"No." His voice was husky as his eyes darkened. "But if we start, I won't want to stop," he warned.

She swallowed and was about to nod her head, when her phone rang.

Closing her eyes, she gathered her thoughts and sighed. His hands dropped from her wrists and he took a step back.

Reaching into her skirt, she pulled out the phone and saw Alex's phone number.

"Hi," she said as she walked towards the windows, buttoning up her blouse. Her reflection shooting back at her showed that her hair was a mess from his hands and she was pretty sure her lips were swollen from his.

"Hi, I'm just calling to let you know that Grant and I can't sing this Thursday. We're heading into Tyler to…" She stopped and said something at one of her kids, then came back. "Sorry, Gavin is going through his terrible twos. Okay, we have to run to Tyler to pick up Laura's new bed. It seems that Gavin decided to use his sister's bed as a trampoline. He broke the frame. It was just lucky that he didn't bust his head in the process. Anyway, we ordered a new frame and it's supposed to be here on Thursday. So…"

"It's okay." She smiled. "I understand. Actually, I was going to call you and let you know that Luke and I are going to sing this week."

"Luke?" Alex must have walked into a more private room because it got really quiet. "Wow, so the rumors are true."

"Rumors?" She turned back to look at Luke, who was still standing by the front door, fully clothed again.

"Sure, I mean, it's all over town that the two of you have been seen walking back to your place every night."

She turned and closed her eyes. "I'd forgotten…"

"Small towns," Alex added. Then she exclaimed, "Is he there now?" When Tessa didn't answer, she groaned. "I interrupted. Sorry. Okay, now I wish we were here Thursday to hear you. I'll get off the phone. Bye." Alex hung up quickly, causing Tessa to chuckle.

"Everything okay?" Luke asked from the doorway.

"Yes," she said, rubbing her head slightly.

Then he was behind her, wrapping his arms around her. "Timing." He sighed into her hair.

"Yeah." She closed her eyes and leaned back, enjoying the sound of his heartbeat.

"I'd better go," he said into her hair.

"No, don't." He turned her around.

"If I stay, we won't stay clothed long," he warned.

Her mouth started watering and she was about to nod in agreement, when he shook his head. "Just like you, I need some time." He dropped his hands. "I think we're set for Thursday." He turned to go.

"Luke, are your parents still married?"

The question stopped him. "Yes. Why?"

She walked over to the sofa and fell back onto the cushions. "I thought my folks were happy. They both acted like they loved one another all the time…" She rested her head back and closed her eyes. "I remember walking into the kitchen and finding them dancing. There wasn't any music playing." She chuckled. "They always said they were dancing to the music in their heads." She released a deep breath and felt the cushions dip next to her and knew he was sitting close.

"And?"

"And." She sat up and looked at him. "This

morning I caught my father sitting on his front porch flirting with my old schoolteacher."

The room was silent for a while, then his laughter broke the silence.

"That's what all this was about?"

She felt her teeth grind as her eyes narrowed. "It's…"

"Flirting. Harmless, from the sound of it."

"So, you think flirting is harmless?"

His laughter died down. "Some flirting is."

"So, if you walked into the diner and saw me sitting in a booth with… John Drake. My hand in his lap…"

She watched his eyes narrow and heat. "That's different."

Her chin rose. "How?"

"Your mother's gone."

Her heart sunk and her breath caught.

"Tessa." He reached for her. "I'm sorry."

She closed her eyes and shook her head. "No. You're right." She tried to steady her breathing after the blow. Even though it was true, just hearing it still upset her.

"Hey." He pulled her closer. "I'm sure it was harmless." His arms wrapped around her.

"Yes," she said into his shoulder. "I'm sure

you're right."

"Hey, how about we head downstairs and grab a beer?"

She laughed and leaned back. "That actually sounds really good."

***

Lucas couldn't remember being more nervous in his life. He'd never played in front of a crowd, and the place was even more crowded tonight than it had been two weeks ago. Apparently, word had gotten out that he and Tessa were doing a duet tonight.

Tessa had warned him that the entire town was gossiping about them being an item. Hell, he didn't care at this point if everyone knew it. After the other night, he was pretty determined to enjoy the relationship ride as long as he could.

Music had opened so much for him. He no longer struggled with nightmares of the accident. Some of the guilt and anger had receded as well.

"Are you nervous?" Tessa asked. She was standing next to him in a soft white lace dress with pink cowgirl boots. He wanted to reach out and wrap his arms around her and take her to the dance floor, but the butterflies in his stomach had glued his feet to the floor.

"Hey." Her soft voice was right next to his ear. He could feel her breath on his skin. Then she was pushing herself up against him as her arms wrapped around his waist. "Focus on me." Her eyes locked with his. "There's only me."

His vision narrowed and soon she was the only person in the crowded room. He could see every shade of brown in her eyes. The fact that there was a streak of gray in each iris, caused him some pleasure. Then he noticed how the lights played over the caramel highlights in her hair. The way her lips puckered and the slight dip in her chin. His fingers reached out and ran over the sexy spot.

"Now, when you're up there, focus on me. Only me," she purred and he couldn't stop himself from nodding in agreement.

Before he knew it, she was handing him the guitar and pushing him towards the stage. It took a moment for his eyes to adjust to the bright lights hitting him, but soon after, he found her in the crowd and smiled. Taking a deep breath, he began to play.

As soon as the first words were out of his mouth, the entire room grew quiet and, even though he knew every eye was on him, his eyes were locked with the only person in the room that mattered to him.

When the song ended, he blinked and chanced a glance around the room, only to realize that every woman's eyes were wet with tears and every man was holding his woman close. There was no polite clapping. Instead, the room exploded with cheers the moment the last chord finished.

His smile was quick and before he knew it, Tessa was standing next to him with her guitar. Her face said everything. Then she was strumming with him and they were singing the duet about how her parents would dance to their own music.

People clapped as they spun around the floor. He was thankful he'd brought a drum track along, since everyone was clapping and stomping in time with the beat.

He felt a bead of sweat roll down his back and, for the first time, he knew exactly what he wanted to do for the rest of his life.

Chapter Ten

He was still running on the natural high a few hours later. There were three empty beer glasses sitting in front of him and two in front of Tessa. Empty shot glasses were scattered around the table.

Alex and Grant hadn't been able to make it, but that didn't stop everyone else he knew from showing up. He was surprised that they all stayed around after he'd sung the last song. They'd called for an encore and he's sung a few classic Johnny Cash songs he knew.

Tessa was pretty much sitting in his lap all night and they had spent a few songs twirling around the dance floor. She'd even spun around once with her father who had shown up just before he'd gone onto the stage. The old man had cried several times during their song. During the other songs, Tessa had wrapped her arms around him.

He'd watched her closely when the old man had taken the school teacher's hand and walked with her to the dance floor for a slower song. Instead of anger, she'd watched them with anxiety. When he pulled her closer, she felt like she was about to jump out of her skin, so, he'd taken her hand and pulled her out on the dance floor, too.

He'd made sure to hold her tight and run his hands over her slowly. He'd rubbed his lips over her collar bone, until he'd felt her body melt next to his. Then he knew she'd forgotten all about her dad dancing with another woman.

To be honest, he'd even forgotten the reason for pulling her onto the dance floor, other than wanting to have her in his arms. Seeing the way her hair caught the lights flashing above them and smelling the perfume on her soft skin flooded him with a desire that outweighed anything else.

His sole purpose for the rest of the night was to see how long he could keep her next to him. When they finally called last call, he was pretty sure he'd found himself not only a new career, but a new purpose as well.

"Walk me home?" Tessa said, leaning on him as they walked out the front door.

"Try and stop me." He smiled down at her and

brushed a strand of her hair aside. She leaned on him and he wrapped his arm around her. "Besides, I parked over there, remember?"

Her smile was her answer. They walked for a moment before she broke the silence. "No one could stop talking about you tonight." She rolled her head back and met his eyes.

"It's your songs they were talking about."

She broke in with a chuckle. "You can't take a compliment." She stopped just under a streetlight and wrapped her arms around him. "You have natural talent. Something I had to work years at"— she shook her head slightly, but the smile remained on her lips— "you just have it." She snapped her fingers.

"Do the years of singing in the shower count?" he joked.

She smiled, then reached up on her toes and placed her lips softly on his. "You were incredible tonight."

He waited a heartbeat. Then, with his arms wrapped around her tightly, he closed his eyes and rested his forehead on hers. "Thanks. You were pretty amazing, too."

She took his hand and continued walking towards her apartment. The entire town of Fairplay was dark and closed down. All the cars from the parking lot had already disappeared. Her apartment was only three blocks away from the Rusty Rail.

With all of the streetlights and the full moon, the town was flooded with light. They walked in silence until they reached the bottom of the stairs.

She didn't even hesitate. She tugged his hand until he was pressed against her. "Are you coming up?" she whispered.

"Are you sure?"

Instead of answering, she tugged on his hand lightly and he followed her up the stairs.

Over the last few days, she'd emptied all the boxes and had finished fixing the place up. He liked the paintings she'd hung on the walls, some of guitars, others of music notes. All of her art had to do with music in one way or another, whether it was hanging guitars or signed drum sticks that were matted and framed behind glass.

When she shut her front door, she didn't stop in the living room, but continued walking back towards the bedroom. For the second time that night, nerves almost overtook him.

She stopped just inside her doorway and wrapped her arms around him. When her lips touched his, all the nerves disappeared. His hands moved to her hips, his nails dug into the soft lace fabric. Her lips were driving him crazy and soon his desire grew and he could hear his heart pounding in his ears.

In one swoop, he moved until she was up against the wall. His fingers pushed until the lacey dress was up past her hips. He stepped between her spread legs and rubbed himself against the silky panties she wore. His fingers dug into her soft skin, then roamed over until he could feel her sweetness.

His mouth had never left hers, but now it dipped lower so he could taste the spot just under her ear. Her fingernails dug into his shoulders as he gently moved aside those silk panties. When he dipped a finger into her heat, she cried out with pleasure and he felt her hips buck.

"My god," he groaned against her neck. The skirt of her dress fell over his hand, so he stepped back quickly and pulled until she stood in front of him clad only in white panties and a matching bra that pushed her perfect breasts together. He wanted to spend the entire night touching and tasting every soft spot.

When he came back to her, he moved one leg until her hips rested on his thigh. His lips claimed hers again as his fingers rubbed the curve of her breasts. He took his time touching, tasting. When he knelt in front of her and pushed those panties aside, he groaned at how beautiful she was.

As he touched her lightly, a soft sound came from her lips and her fingers dug into his hair, holding him tight.

He rubbed his fingers over her until he felt her legs tense, and then, when he couldn't deny the desire to taste her, he leaned forward and ran his tongue over her soft lips.

He kissed the insides of her thighs and rubbed his mouth over every tender spot until her knees buckled. Standing, he lifted her gently into his arms and walked across the room to lay her softly on her bedspread.

Looking down at her, he knew he'd lost more than his mind just wanting to be with her. He'd never felt so strongly about making sure a woman was pleased before. Now, it was his only purpose to make sure she had every desire she'd ever wanted.

***

Lucas looked down at her after he'd done the most wonderful things to her, and she felt her entire body react to his gaze. Her nipples peaked when his eyes moved slowly over her bra. Between her legs grew damp when his eyes traveled lower.

When he moved slowly onto the bed, still fully clothed, she propped herself up on her elbows.

"How about you lose some of those clothes?" Her own eyes moved over him.

He'd looked damn sexy all night in his worn jeans, black boots, and black T-shirt. He'd been wearing a black Stetson all night, but had lost it just inside her doorway. His hair was messy from her hands, and there was light stubble covering his face, making him look a little dangerous and a whole lot sexier.

"In due time." His smile made her glad she was not trusting her legs to keep her upright.

He reached up and tugged on her remaining clothes until she was lying in front of him completely naked. When she tried to kick off her boots, he stopped her.

"No, leave them." That smile was something she could get caught up in. Honestly, it was hard to deny him anything when that dimple of his winked at the side of his mouth.

"I think it's only fair that you remove one article of clothing." She wanted to cross her arms over her chest, but the way his eyes were soaking her up made all her shyness disappear.

He leaned back and flipped his shirt over his head. That's what she'd been wanting, her hands on his skin. To see those sexy muscles of his jerk when she ran a fingertip over them.

"Hmmm." She held him still as her hands played over him slowly. His eyes closed and his head fell back when her fingers followed the sexy trail of dark hair that disappeared below his jeans.

She'd never seen a man with a true six-pack. When she ran a fingertip over each line, the muscles bunched and his breath hitched.

"Am I hurting you?" she asked, her eyes rushing to his.

His low chuckle caused his stomach muscles to move again in a different way. She found it totally fascinating and wanted to have it happen again.

"No, darling. You're killing me." He circled her wrists with his hands, then moved until she was pinned under him, his bare chest against hers. She'd lost all her ability to breathe and think. She'd thought that her nipples had gotten hard under his gaze. That was nothing compared to having his warm skin brush up against hers.

He pushed a thigh between her legs and when the denim of his jeans brushed against her private spot, she closed her eyes and couldn't stop herself from moving her hips.

"Yes, that's it," he groaned next to her ear as his mouth caused more goosebumps all over her skin. "Ride me." He flexed his hips. His hand locked hers above her head as the other slowly roamed over her. When his fingers pinched her nipple lightly, her hips jerked off the mattress and she pressed herself more firmly against his jeans.

Her legs wrapped around his hips as his fingers spread her once more and he dipped a finger into her wetness. She couldn't stop the cry from breaking from her lips, nor could she have ever dreamed that with his simple touch, he'd take her to a place she'd only imagined.

"Come for me," he growled as his mouth covered her breast. "Let go." His mouth traveled down her belly until his lips once more covered her sex. When he placed his tongue where his fingers were moments ago, she did let go. Completely.

She was floating and spinning all at once. She was pretty sure even her back wasn't touching the mattress anymore. All she could feel was his skin against hers. She could only hear the beating of her heart pounding in her ears and she tasted… him.

Her eyes fluttered open when his weight lifted from her.

"No."

"Easy." He chuckled. "Just removing my pants."

She found the strength to watch him. He kept his eyes focused on her as he removed his boots, then peeled those sexy worn jeans from his hips.

When his sex sprang free, she held her breath and fought off the desire to run and call the whole night a mistake. Instead, she watched him crawl back onto the bed towards her. When he ripped open the condom, she realized her body was already wanting his.

Deciding to let her body take over, she closed her eyes as he moved over her. Biting her bottom lip, she waited for the pain she knew would be coming, but instead, he started kissing her neck once more.

"You taste so sweet," he said next to her ear. "I love this soft spot… here… and here…" He ran his mouth up her neck and over to the other side to do the same. His hands moved slowly over her, igniting flames everywhere he went.

"Lucas," she moaned. Her fingers were digging into his shoulders.

"Look at me." He moved back. "I want to see your eyes go soft when I enter you."

Her eyes slid open and for a moment she thought she was going to cry when she noticed the tenderness there.

He leaned down and brushed his lips over hers before his hips flexed slightly. She did feel a burst of slight pain, but it was quickly overcome by joy at being closer to anyone than she'd ever been before. Her legs wrapped around his, holding him to her.

He grew still until she moved her hips. Then he closed his eyes and dove deep into her as his kisses grew more urgent.

She'd never felt anything like being this close to Luke before. His skin heated next to her own burning skin. She felt the slap of his body next to hers and his mouth pleasured hers until finally she felt herself building once more. Just as she was about to jump over the edge, she heard him growl, "Yes, come for me," again.

"Luke," she cried out as she felt herself spinning once more. She felt him stiffen above her and heard him growl out her name and knew she would never feel regret about that night. About letting Lucas James be her first.

Chapter Eleven

Luke was trying to process what the hell had just happened. His heart rate was still way above normal and he was pretty sure he'd just broken a ton of moral rules. He wasn't willing to dwell on that just yet.

"Why didn't you tell me?" he finally asked once he'd caught his breath.

"Hmmm?" She wrapped her arms around his shoulders once more. They had fallen flat on the mattress but were now roaming his back, causing him to stir once more.

Instead of enjoying the feeling, he pulled away and looked down at her. "That this... that I was... your first."

She was smiling up at him and just the sight of her hair fanned out on the pillow was causing him to grow hard again.

"Why would I? Besides, I had the feeling that if you knew"—her arms pulled him back down to her— "you wouldn't have let this happen." She leaned up and kissed him until he melted back down into her arms.

"Damn straight," he said without any energy. "You deserve… better for your first…"

She chuckled. "Better than the best?" She wrapped her legs around him once more.

"Careful, you might give me a big head," he joked.

"I don't see you having that problem." She pulled on his shoulder until he came back down and covered her. His hips started moving on their own and before he knew it, he was fighting for breath once more.

"I can't stop myself… around you," he growled into her hair as she rained kisses down his neck.

"Good." Her nails were scrapping his sides, driving him nuts. He rolled her hips up until he gripped her tight butt. When he felt her convulse around him and heard her cry out again, only then did he let himself go once more.

He must have slept, since the sunlight in his face woke him. Her body was tangled in his. Her sexy legs wrapped around his hip and her hair was next to his face. Her face was squished against his chest. He enjoyed the feeling of her breathing, her entire body rising and falling with each breath. He counted the breaths, then counted her heartbeats against his.

Closing his eyes, he wished he could stay the entire day here, with her. Unfortunately, he had Chase and Lauren's bull being delivered later that morning.

Glancing at the clock, he figured he had enough time to enjoy a shower with Tessa, and maybe head downstairs for a cup of coffee and one of Holly's cinnamon rolls.

When he moved, Tessa tried to snuggle deeper into his chest. He solved the problem by simply picking her up and carrying her to the bathroom with him.

He stopped just inside the doorway and whistled.

"Hmmm?" She pushed her hair out of her eyes and looked up at him.

"Nice digs." He smiled down at her. "I'm going to have to take notes for when I remodel my bathroom."

She chuckled. "This is the reason I decided to move here, instead of in the small house with dad. Besides..." He felt her stiffen, but didn't give her time to stress about her father's love life. Instead, he walked towards the shower and stepped in, then

155

reached to turn on the spray.

"It's cold!" She screamed and tried to get out of his arms.

"Course it is. How else are you going to wake up?" He chuckled and released her until she stood on her own.

She reached for the knobs, only to have him turn her around and hold her against the stone wall. "No, it's perfect." He chuckled when she tried to kick out. Giving her no time, he dipped his head and kissed her until there was steam coming from both of their bodies.

"Someone could get hurt like that," she said, as she dried her hair with a towel.

"You've got those sticky things on the floor." He pulled on his jeans and hunted for his shirt. "Besides, those handles on the wall come in real handy." He heard her laugh.

"I'd never thought about using them... quite like that before."

He glanced over his shoulder towards her. "No, but I bet you won't forget it now."

She shook her head and then pulled on a shirt to hide the blush. But he'd seen her cheeks turn pink and couldn't stop the smile, knowing he'd caused it.

When they walked down the stairs and into Holly's, hand in hand, he tried to convince her to spend the day with him at his place.

"We could go riding until you have to come into work."

She calculated. "I'm off Fridays and Saturdays."

"You are?"

"Yes, this week. I switched with someone so I didn't have to drag my butt in after last night." She waved at the blonde behind the counter.

"Perfect." He stopped her from walking further into the place. "So, spend the day with me. We'll take a ride, have a picnic, then..." He whispered in her ear until the pink returned to her cheeks.

"Well, are you two coming or going?" Holly said from behind the counter. "Before you decide, I've got a fresh pan of cinnamon rolls that just came out of the oven."

"Coming!" they both said at the same time. They laughed and walked towards the bar area.

"So... last night happened," Holly said, leaning against the counter. "Don't get me wrong, I love my husband with every ounce of being, but... damn." She fluttered her eyelashes at him and chuckled. "Boy, you've got some lungs."

He didn't know what to say. Actually, he'd seen the woman and her husband enjoying themselves last night. Travis Nolan was one of the men around town he hardly knew anything about. He'd actually only seen the man once or twice.

"Um… thanks, I think." Now it was his turn to blush. He turned to the menu and focused on picking out a coffee instead.

After they ordered, they picked a table and waited for their coffee and cinnamon rolls to be delivered.

"She was just joking with you," Tessa added as she reached for his hands.

"I know." He shifted, and glanced around and she chuckled. "What?"

"Nothing. I think it's cute that you get embarrassed."

"I'm not…" She stopped him by raising her eyebrows. "Okay, maybe a little. I've heard what her husband does… did for a living. Not to mention what her father did. I've actually read his book. Um, her book." He frowned and tilted his head.

"Her book, about her father. His notes and poems are in it, but she wrote it. She's actually writing another one."

"Oh?" He leaned forward. He'd really enjoyed the first book.

"About her husband," she added. He waited until after their food and drinks were delivered.

"Thanks, Karlene," Tessa said, then reached for her mug.

"Isn't her name April?" He frowned after the blonde.

"No, April is her sister. She works here too."

"Oh." He shrugged and reached for his coffee.

"You really don't know that many people in town, do you?"

He shrugged again. "Not yet. I'm getting there."

She tilted her head. "How long have you lived here?"

He calculated as he bit into the hot roll but lost his train of thought when the sugary goodness melted in his mouth. "Damn!" He groaned. "This is almost as good as last night... and this morning." He winked at her, causing her to blush once more. "I like doing that."

She turned beet read. "What?" She almost coughed it out.

"Making you blush," he joked. He knew what she was thinking and didn't mind.

"Oh." She reached for her roll and he watched her eyes roll and close with pleasure. "Well, why have you avoided meeting people?" she asked after a moment of silence.

"I haven't avoided it... per se." He took another bite of his roll.

"No?" She sighed. "What's the clerks name at the Grocery Stop?" He shrugged. "How about the

159

owner of the hardware store?" He shrugged again. "What about the gas attendant?" Upon his blank stare, she shook her head. "Do you know anyone in town besides the one's I've introduced you to?"

He thought about it. "I know Mama."

"She doesn't really count. She makes a point to know everyone."

He chuckled. "Okay, how about Grant. I've had him and his father come out and check up on my herd."

She nodded. "Yes, I suppose that counts."

"Oh, I cut my finger pretty deep on the barbed fence a few weeks after moving in and met... Merissa? At the clinic. She's married to... Ryan?"

"Melissa. She goes by Missy. She's married to Reece, who is Ryan's twin."

"Okay, now you're just confusing me." He laughed.

"I guess I can see how you'd get confused."

"I've been wondering why you hang out with people a few years older than you, rather than the people in town your own age." He finished off his roll and took the last sip of his coffee.

"No reason," she said, but he knew she was hiding something. Just then, the door opened and Alex rushed in. When she spotted them, she rushed over.

160

***

"I didn't..." Alex started, then stopped, held up a finger, and leaned on her knees to take several deep breaths.

"What?" Tessa instantly worried. "Is something wrong?" She started to get up from the table.

"No," Alex shook her head then pulled up a chair and sat next to them. "Oh, are those cinnamon rolls?" She glanced at Tessa's almost empty plate. Pushing the plate towards Alex, she waited until her friend shoved the last bite into her mouth. "Thanks, I ran all the way from Mama's."

Tessa laughed. "It's only two blocks."

"Uh, yeah. Try doing that after having two kids." She held up her fingers close to Tessa's eyes. "Two!"

Tessa smiled. "Okay, do you need some water or some oxygen?"

Alex smirked at her and narrowed her eyes. "You just wait... someday..."

"Was there something you had to tell us?" Tessa burst in.

"Oh!" A huge smile flooded Alex's face. "Okay, first let me premise this with the fact that it wasn't really my fault. Since I couldn't be there last night, I asked Haley to record... you know, so I could see how it went..."

"Um..." Tessa shook her head, not quite

understanding.

"Well, anyway, since the file was too large to email, and I still haven't figure out how to do that whole share thingie…" She rolled her eyes. "Wes figured out how to put the video up on YouTube. So, by the time I finally made it into Mama's this morning and logged into my iPad…" She glanced around. "Damn." She looked towards the door where her husband was walking in, holding a child in each arm and a large diaper bag over his shoulders. He was frowning and smiling at the same time.

"Oh!" Alex rushed over to him, took her iPad from the diaper bag, and kissed him solidly on his lips. "Thanks!"

Grant nodded, then turned and walked back out the door.

"Would you mind telling me what is going on?" Tessa asked, only to have Alex turn to Luke.

"I hope it's okay… I mean… You're a hit."

"What?" He frowned over at her and Tessa could tell he was as confused as she was.

Instead of answering, Alex opened up her iPad, logged in to the Wi-Fi, and hit play.

There on the screen was Luke singing her song last night. Even in the darkness of the room, his entire body was lit up. Since the entire crowd was silent, his voice rang clear.

Goosebumps grew all over Tessa as she listened to the entire song. By the time it was over, there were tears sliding down her face.

"It's beautiful." Alex sighed. She reached over and hit pause. "And has over a hundred-thousand views."

"What!" Tessa looked at the screen and sure enough, they were quickly approaching the hundred and fifty thousand mark. "Oh my…"

"I…" Luke shook his head.

"The duet of you two has almost as many."

Tessa was really critical about her own performance, but tried hard not to focus on her own voice. Instead, she focused on Luke's. The number under that video shocked her, too.

"I… I don't understand." She shook her head.

"You're an overnight hit," Alex said, smiling big.

Her eyes moved over to Luke. His color had paled and he actually looked a little sick.

"Luke?" She reached for him.

"I…" He shook his head. "I have to go… the bull." He quickly got up and rushed from the room.

"I…" Alex frowned. "I didn't mean…"

"I think he's just a little shocked. He's so shy." She patted Alex's hand and rushed outside, but

163

Luke's truck had already disappeared around the corner.

"I'm sorry, Tessa." Alex walked out and stood beside her. "I didn't mean for anyone else to see it. Only me."

She smiled at Alex. "It's okay. Really," she said as she bit her bottom lip with worry.

Chapter Twelve

Chase had dropped off the bull named Roger, which, oddly, suited the thing perfectly. Five minutes after being released into the pen with all his heifers, the darn thing had rolled in the mud pit left over from last week's rain. He looked like he'd enjoyed every minute of it.

Luke sat on the fence and watched the cattle get to know one another. The scene from the coffee shop played over and over in his mind. So many emotions flooded him. Nerves, fear, anger. He didn't know why he was angry.

It wasn't as if Alex had meant to give away Tessa's songs. His mind played over numbers. If she'd been paid each time someone had listened to her songs, she'd have enough money to stop

165

working at the diner. Hell, maybe even enough for her to live comfortably, if she could secure a deal because of it.

He didn't know much about the legal aspects of things. Since it was on YouTube, did that mean she had given up her rights to the songs?

And how did he feel about people watching him sing? Sure, he'd played in front of about a hundred people in the Rusty Rail, but he'd never imagined anything close to a hundred thousand. No way. Never.

He was determined to go inside and do a little research on the internet when he heard the car turn down his drive. He frowned when he saw Tessa's sedan. His heart sank slightly and he felt guilty for leaving the coffee shop like he had.

"Are you okay?" she asked once she'd gotten out of the car. She'd changed from her shorts and shirt into a pair of long jeans and a long-sleeved flannel riding shirt. Even her dusty boots said she had been planning on going riding. Her hair was tied back with a blue ribbon.

"I'm fine. How are you?" He reached for her and she walked into his arms.

"I'm okay." She chuckled a little.

"I'm sorry," he blurted out.

"For?" She waited.

He released a breath, then shook his head. "I

guess, for everything."

"Luke, are you mad at me?"

"No!" He took her closer into his arms. "Of course not. Why would I be?"

"Haley and Alex didn't mean any harm."

"I know." He brushed away a strand of hair that had blown in her eyes.

"Are you... upset? Embarrassed? What?" She leaned back and dropped her arms. After a moment of silence, she stomped her foot lightly and added, "Luke, talk to me."

"I... I thought you'd be upset. I'm sorry I left. I was just... I don't know." He walked over and blindly watched the cows playing in the fields. "I guess I'm scared you're going to be upset that you didn't make a deal."

"A deal?" She walked over and leaned against the fence next to him. "What are you talking about?"

"A deal with your agent. I mean, so many people have your song now. And you still aren't getting paid for the first few songs."

She shocked him by bending over and laughing, hard and long. She didn't stop until he put a hand on her shoulder.

"You... here I was, worried that we'd upset you by having you become the sexiest cowboy singer ever recorded and here you are... worried that I'm

167

not getting paid for the songs I wrote." She smiled up at him and he pretty much lost what it was he was trying to stress.

"Um…" He shook his head.

"Luke. You're nuts, you know that." She walked over and turned him until he was facing her. "Don't worry about me. Enjoy your stardom."

She stood back and smiled at him. "After you left, I got a call from my agent."

"And?" He held in his excitement.

"And, he's decided who's going to sing my songs."

He waited, holding his breath. "Who?"

"You." She leaned up and brushed a kiss on his lips.

"Me?" He stepped back, but realized the fence was right behind him.

"Yes. He's coming down next week to listen to you sing, live. If he likes what he hears, he has a few record companies that are willing to sign you."

"Me?" he asked again, shaking his head.

"Yes, you. That is… if you enjoyed singing on stage and liked singing my songs and want to keep doing it."

"I love singing your songs." He closed his eyes and enjoyed the feeling of her rubbing her body against his. "I loved singing." When his eyes

168

opened, he couldn't stop himself from smiling back at her. "So, that means, you'll finally get paid for your songs?"

She nodded. "And you'll get paid for singing them. Not to mention having every girl swooning over your sexy voice, face, and this"—she reached around and grabbed his butt— "sexy body."

His smile slipped a little. He hadn't thought about who else had seen the video. His stomach instantly rolled.

"Hey." Her voice broke into his dark thoughts. "Are you okay?" she asked, her voice laced with concern.

Nodding his head, he glanced off towards the field. "How about a ride? It'll help clear my head." He nodded towards the corral and his horses. "Lightning is pretty old, but he can keep up with Tex."

"Which one is Lightning and which one is Tex?" She dropped her arms and walked over to the corral to look at the horses.

"Tex is the black one with the white star between his eyes. Lightning is the brown one with the white bolt between his eyes."

She laughed. "What about the cream-colored one?"

"That's Ace. She's moody." He stuck his booted foot on the bottom rung. "I haven't been able to put a saddle on her yet or get near her for that

169

matter."

"Oh?" Tessa turned to him. "What'll you give me if I could?"

He shook his head. "I don't think you should try. She bites."

"So do I." Tessa winked then crawled between the fence railings. He was about to jump the fence, when Ace rushed towards Tessa like they were old friends.

Tessa reached out her arms and Ace walked right into them, gently rubbing her head against Tessa's hair as Tessa laughed. "I've missed you too, Speedy." She leaned up and kissed the horse right on the lips.

He stood there like he'd been struck by lightning.

Crawling through the fence, he walked over to the pair, shaking his head. "Well, damn. You are full of surprises." He reached out towards the horse, then hesitated.

"Speedy, this is Luke. He's the boss now." The horse glanced between him and Tessa, then dipped her head in what he could only assume was acknowledgement. "She doesn't like the name Ace," she said as he reached his hand out and pat the horse.

"I can see that." He laughed when the horse rubbed her face against his shoulder.

"She also loves sugar cubes. So always come prepared." Tessa pulled several out of her jean pockets and gave each horse some. "Now…" She dusted off her hands and turned to him. "How about that ride?"

***

"I can't believe you bought Speedy." She petted the horse's mane and took a deep breath. It felt so good to be back in the saddle.

"Well, the man said that the horse had never really liked anyone… except—"

"Me. I used to sneak into Mr. Walker's fields every day. Speedy was my only friend growing up. I remember the day she was born." She glanced over at him. "I skipped school that day and spent the entire day with her and her mother."

"Where did you get the name Speedy?"

She laughed. "How about I show you?" She kicked her heels into the horse's flanks and the horse bolted. He stood back and watched for a moment, before kicking Tex into following them.

The fact that the she'd beat him to the fence line by almost two hundred yards, not only impressed him, but told him he'd seriously underestimated his own horse.

"Damn," he said, a little winded. "Either that's the fastest horse in the county or you're one hell of a rider."

171

She laughed. "Both, I think." She slid off the horse and started slowly walking along the fence line.

He followed suit and fell into step with her.

"So, you're really okay with me singing your songs? What about Clint Black or Garth Brooks?"

She laughed. "They were never going to make a deal with them. Most of the big names write their own songs now." She stopped and turned towards him. "Besides, maybe soon, you'll be as big as they are."

"I don't think—"

"Luke, trust me, you're easily as good as them and the world could use a new cowboy to drool over." She started walking again. "Just promise me one thing." She glanced over her shoulder at him. "Remember the little folks when you're famous."

He laughed. "Right." He glanced off towards his house. "I'm just starting to finally feel like I fit in here. I don't think I'd like heading back to the city anytime soon."

"You never know." She sighed and glanced around. "I never thought I'd come back to Fairplay, and here I am."

He thought about it. "No, if I've learned one thing this last year, it's that I'm done with the city life."

She smiled. "Yeah, I like it once in a while, but

172

after about a week, the traffic just pisses me off."

He laughed. "That and the smell."

"Then there's the crime," she joked and they continued to list off things they hated about city life.

By the time they climbed back on the horses, he'd forgotten all about his worry of who would find out about him singing. After all, sooner or later, his family was bound to find him. He wasn't really worried about them; it was Kristen's family he was more worried about.

The ride was just what he needed. That and the time with Tessa.

"Stay for dinner?" he asked as they were brushing down the horses.

"Can you cook?" she teased as she looked over Speedy's neck.

"Not really, but I can make do. I was going to toss on some burgers... or I have some steaks," he added when he remembered Chase had dropped off a bundle of meat when he'd delivered the bull.

"Mmm, steak sounds good." She glanced over and giggled. "Looks like Roger likes it here."

He glanced out the fence and noticed the bull mounting one of his heifers. "He should, for what I'm paying for him."

"Ohhh, does that make him a gigolo?" She giggled and he found the sound completely erotic.

173

Dropping the brush, he walked over and took her hands, setting aside the brush she held. "If you like"—he dipped his head and brushed his lips across those soft ones of hers— "we can watch the show before dinner."

She smiled. "Maybe we can make our own entertainment?"

He couldn't explain the amount of desire that flooded his system at that moment, but all of a sudden, he had her pinned to the side of the stall, her mouth crushed under his, her body pushed tight up against his desire.

"Tessa." He dropped his head until their foreheads rested against one another. "I can't seem to get enough of you."

"Good," she said, taking his face until he looked up at her. "Because I'm willing to give you as much as you can take." She smiled. "Deal?"

He nodded, feeling the knot in his throat. "Deal."

Chapter Thirteen

Dinner was perfect. They sat on his back porch and grilled the steaks as the sun sank lower in the sky. When it became too dark to see, he flipped a switch and several dozen rows of lights flickering above them on the terrace.

The fireflies buzzed around in the yard and the sound of the country surrounded them. She couldn't have asked for a more perfect night.

"Stay," he said, reaching for her hand as they finished dinner.

Instead of answering, she dipped her head and smiled at him.

When he took her hand and led her into the house, her insides jumped. Even though they had made love three times before, she was still nervous for tonight.

His bedroom was near the back and was easily twice the size as hers. She had seen the main rooms when they had walked in, but here, in his bedroom, things were a little more updated. He'd obviously painted and had put in new hardwood flooring. Everything looked fresh and updated.

She was dying to say something about it, but he leaned down and kissed her and she lost all train of thought. As before, he took his time peeling off her clothing. This time, however, instead of easily pulling off a dress, he had to kneel before her and yank off her riding boots and then her jeans, which were a little snug. She took her time following him and pulling off his boots. His jeans were a little looser than the night before and easily slid down his legs.

She hadn't really had time to explore him much, so she took this time to run her hands over his thighs and calves. There was a light dusting of dark hair over him that she found completely sexy.

When her fingers brushed against his boxer briefs, he twitched and she wanted to slide the last barrier off him.

He stopped her by pulling her up as he circled her wrists once more. "My turn," he said, turning her around until the backs of her legs hit his bed.

He smiled, then with one finger, pushed against

her chest until she fell backwards. She laughed as she fell. Then he was on top of her and she lost her breath.

He kissed her until her hips moved on their own, grinding against his shorts until her panties were almost soaked.

He pulled back and ran his mouth over her, down her belly as he slid her panties off her legs slowly. His hands shifted her legs up until her feet were flat on his mattress and her knees were spread wide. When he settled between them, she couldn't stop the moan from escaping, nor could she stop her hips from jerking off the bed.

One of his hands moved up and pressed on her belly, keeping her down on the mattress. His other hand moved until she felt a finger slide into her as his tongue did wonders to other parts of her. She felt herself slide into one of the easiest releases she'd ever experienced.

When he tried to shift, she closed her legs and flipped him over in one swift move.

"My turn," she said back to him. He was smiling up at her. Her fingers circled his wrists and pulled them above his head. "Play fair."

He shook his head. "It's too fun to be bad."

She smiled back down at him. "For a while?"

When he nodded, she leaned down and repeated everything he'd done to her, but when she pulled his shorts down, she hesitated.

"You don't have to…" he said, starting to move.

"No, I want…" She licked her lips, then looked up at him and met his eyes. "Tell me if I do something wrong." He nodded quickly and she dipped her head down to take him fully into her mouth.

He was smoother than she'd ever imagined. Lace over steel. She'd always wondered what they'd meant by it, and now she knew. She took her time enjoying him, exploring him, until she felt his hips jerk and she was being pushed quickly under him.

She heard him slip on the condom moments before his hips jerked and he was fully embedded into her. She cried out with excitement as he started to move, his mouth close to her ear.

"You little devil." She growled. "You're… too… damn… sexy…" He grunted between each word, sending waves of desire flooding through her.

Wrapping her legs around him, she locked her ankles and held on as he started moving faster. She was breathless when she cried out his name and heard him groan hers at the same time.

She lay in his arms, once more listening to his heart settle in his chest. There was something so intimate about her head rising and falling with each one of his breaths. About feeling him curled next to her after spending the day together, enjoying their conversations and having some damn great sex. She'd never experienced any of that with a man before.

It was funny, even though he'd found out she had been a virgin, he hadn't made fun of her or joked with her about it. Instead, he'd been concerned. Worried that he hadn't shown her enough tenderness.

Which only made her love him even more. That thought stopped her and she clenched tight.

"You okay?" he asked easily.

"Sure," she lied. "Umm. Bathroom?" she asked, needing just a moment.

"There." He started to get up.

"No, I can find it." She jumped up and grabbed some clothes as she headed out.

Making sure she flipped the lock, she rested her head against the door and took a couple deep breathes.

She can't be in love! Not that it was impossible, but it just wasn't... probable. She'd convinced herself it would never happen, years ago.

After all, she was Tracy Bracey. Greasy Tracy. Tracy... She stopped herself from listing more than a dozen names she'd been called over the years.

She flipped on the lights, splashed water in her face, and looked deep into her own brown eyes,

179

something she'd done since first reading *Anne of Green Gables*. Oh, she never called her reflection Katie, but she did imagine she could look deep into her soul and find out more about herself.

In love, she repeated silently. She couldn't be in love. But looking into her eyes, she knew instantly that it was true.

Her entire essence had changed. Even her eyes were different. Her skin glowed. Her entire being was... different.

For the first time in her life, she looked at herself in the mirror and thought she was beautiful. Not just beautiful but... sexy. Like Luke had told her moments before.

She stood back and looked at herself completely.

She was holding the clothes to her chest and dropped them and took a long, hard look at herself. She was beautiful. She was sexy.

Her long brown hair was no longer greasy and instead shined in the light. It was a little tangled from Luke's hands, but for the most part, it was beautiful. Her hips were fuller than they had ever been. She'd been such a skinny child, even her teachers had assumed she was anorexic. It was hard to tell everyone that it was hard to eat when you were so depressed.

Her breasts had even finally filled out to a solid C cup. Perfect for her body frame. She watched her reflection as she thought about Luke and what he'd done to her body moments before. Her nipples puckered and her skin began to glow.

"Yup, definitely love," she said out loud.

"Did you say something?" Luke called to her.

Instantly, her checks turned pink. "No, um…" She bit her bottom lip. Then she decided that if she was woman enough to have sex, she was woman enough to confess her feelings to him.

Marching to the door, she flung it open and was about to blurt it out when she burst out laughing.

He was standing just outside the door, butt naked, his ear to the door. When she opened the door, he flung his arms backwards and fell on his butt.

"Were you eavesdropping on me?"

"Me? No!" He did a move that she'd never seen before and was instantly up on the balls of his feet. "I was… Um, making sure you were okay."

She laughed again. "Right." She crossed her arms over her chest and looked down at him.

He cleared his throat. "Well, is everything okay?"

She smiled and nodded. And understood that when the right time came to tell him, she would know. So, instead of spilling her heart to him, she bit her tongue and nodded towards the bathroom. "Feel like breaking in your shower?"

He laughed, and when his eyes met hers, the smile fell away and he grabbed her hips and pushed her into the bathroom, following her closely.

***

Luke flipped the pancake and glanced up when Tessa walked into the kitchen the next morning.

"Hungry?" he asked.

"Boy, am I." She leaned against the counter and closed her eyes. "Are those pecan pancakes?"

He nodded. "Bacon and eggs, too."

"Wow, I've never had a man make me breakfast before." She took the glass of OJ he offered her.

"There's a lot you haven't had men do for you before." He leaned closer and brushed his lips over hers. "Someday we'll have to talk about that."

She nodded and swallowed a sip of juice. "Someday we will." She turned and walked to the back door.

"Looks like Roger still has enough energy this morning."

"Yeah, he was still going at it when I woke up." He shook his head. "A man's gotta eat and sleep sometime."

She chuckled.

"Do you have plans today?" she asked.

"I have some chores around here, but nothing big. You?" He glanced over at her.

"I'm heading into Tyler to pick up a few things for the apartment." He waited, holding his breath. "Would you like to come with me?"

He took the last pancake off the burner and turned to her. "I was hoping you'd ask." He set the plate on the table, then held out a chair for her.

"Good, because I'm in desperate need of a truck."

"Oh?"

"Yeah, I'm getting a new dresser and it's… big. Bigger than my car." She waited.

He laughed. "What was your plan to get it home in the first place?"

"To talk you into driving up there with me." She smiled.

"Tell you what…" He leaned closer to her. "If you help me muck out the stalls and feed the cattle, I'll drive you into Tyler and we can pick up your dresser and have dinner."

"How about stopping by my place first for a shower and a change?"

"Can I join you for the shower?" He reached over and took her hand.

"I was counting on it." Her cheeks flushed and he couldn't imagine spending the day any other way than seeing the look of heat in her brown eyes.

Chores went a whole lot faster with the two of them working together. He was impressed that Tessa wasn't a wimp when it came to mucking out the stalls in the barn. She didn't complain about carrying bales of hay to the field, either.

By the time they drove into town towards her place, he was seriously looking forward to the shower. He'd tossed a change of clothes into the back of his truck.

He took his time making love to her in the shower, making sure she reached pleasure twice before taking his own.

"I could get used to this," she purred when they were back on the road, heading towards Tyler.

"Mucking out stalls?" He glanced towards her and watched her smile.

"That, and having someone make me breakfast and…" She sighed. "Long, lazy showers."

He smiled, took her hand in his, and carried it to his lips. "So could I."

The rest of the day went smoothly. They picked up her dresser, a long classic country one painted the same color as the cabinets in her kitchen.

He drove her to his favorite barbeque place, Stanley's. A band had just started playing on the small stage area outside, and they enjoyed good food and great music.

As they drove back to town, he wondered aloud how they were going to get the dresser up the stairs and into her bedroom by themselves.

"Billy and Savannah are coming over tomorrow to help carry it upstairs," she answered as they pulled in.

"Will it be okay parked here?" He stopped just outside the parking lot.

She laughed. "This is Fairplay, not Houston."

"Just the same, I'm backing in so it will be hidden better."

"So, can I take that to mean that you're staying the night?" She leaned closer to him.

"If you'll have me." He wrapped his arm around her and pulled her halfway into his lap.

"Oh, I'll have you. Several different ways." He felt the words vibrate and got hard instantly.

"If you're not careful, one of those ways will be in a dark parking lot, on the front seat of my truck."

She giggled. "I've never done it in a car…" She didn't get another word out because he'd crushed her lips under his.

He didn't remember removing her clothes, but suddenly, she was straddling him, her jeans tossed on the floor. She'd unzipped him, and had him in her hands, causing his breath to hitch.

When he pulled the condom from his back pocket, she took it from his hands and gently pushed it on him, which almost killed him. Then she was hovering back over him and sliding slowly down on his full length.

Her lips burned a trail down his neck and he was pretty sure he wasn't going to be able to stop himself from coming quickly. He forced himself to wait until he felt her tighten around him before letting himself fall.

Chapter Fourteen

By that next Thursday, he had learned two more of her songs. She'd written a few more that week, but said they weren't ready yet.

So he found himself once more standing by the stage at the Rusty Rail, nerves picking at him, with Tessa by his side. He knew he could make it through the night because he'd done it before and he knew the rush that came after.

The place was packed. There were three high-rollers dressed in suits whom Tessa had been talking to when he'd walked in the door. She introduced them all, but he was still unsure who was whom and what exactly they did. All he knew was that if things went well tonight, her songs would finally be making her money. Which only

187

made him more nervous. Oh, and the fact that they wanted him to sing them all. That caused him some trouble as well.

But he'd been doing a lot of thinking about it and he was determined to continue singing. Even if things didn't go well with the high-rollers.

When he walked onto the stage, the place erupted. This time, his eyes traveled around the crowd. There were twice as many people as last week. When he started strumming the guitar, his eyes moved to Tessa's and focused.

He played her newest songs first, then played the one's from last week. It was strange to hear the crowd sing along with the chorus, but it helped him relax and have a little more fun. He even caught himself dancing around the stage a little more.

When he finally walked off the stage after half a dozen songs, there was a bead of sweat dripping down his back and he had to remove his hat to swipe his forehead.

Instantly, he was engulfed by the crowd. He searched for Tessa as people walked up and slapped him on his back or asked for pictures with him.

It was all a little crazy. When he felt Tessa's hand take his, he relaxed and felt a little easier about the entire thing.

"So?" he asked when, finally, they found a quiet

corner. "Did they say anything?" He nodded to the three men still standing at the bar.

"How does a trip to Houston for a week sound?" Her smile grew huge.

"Houston?"

She wrapped her arms around his neck. "They want to sign a record deal with you." It almost came out as a squeal.

"Me?" he choked out.

She laughed. "They want to record in two weeks."

"Isn't that fast? I mean…"

"There is one condition." She frowned slightly. "They want me to sing two songs with you and we'll have to come up with four more songs before then, besides the one's you sang tonight."

"Four… Houston?" He shook his head, trying to process everything.

She laughed and hugged him. It felt so good that he spun her around. At that moment he knew that, no matter what it took, he'd do anything to make her smile and look at him the way she was now.

***

The next two weeks flew by. Tessa had never spent so much time writing before. Her fingers were cramped and she was sure she'd get blocked, but with Luke by her side, she pushed through it all. She'd written the four new songs they wanted plus one more, just in case they didn't like one.

She and Luke worked day and night to refine each one. Some nights, he would crash at her place, other's she would stay at his place and help him care for the animals, including his dog Lucky, whom she had instantly fallen in love with. When they stayed at her place the little dog came along.

She found it adorable that he brought along the dog bed for Lucky and some of her toys. She joked with him about needing a small dog carrier to tote her around in.

She hadn't had much time to finish decorating her apartment, nor did she have as much time to be with her father. But, according to him and everyone else in town, he was spending more and more time with Martha Cole.

It seemed like they were quickly becoming an item. She hadn't had a lot of time to process her feelings about it. Every time she talked to Luke about it, he would assure her that it was no big deal.

She kept wanting to be hurt that her father had moved on so quickly after her mother's death, but she had to admit that he looked happier. He'd gained a few pounds, which made him look younger somehow.

Chase had stopped by and picked up Roger,

who looked completely satisfied that he'd enjoyed every one of Luke's heifers. He'd made arrangements for Chase to watch the rest of his animals while they were gone, but decided to take Lucky along with them to Houston. To be honest, he was finding it harder to part with the little girl. Besides, she loved listening to the music and he figured she wouldn't get in the way. Much.

"In a few months, you should have more than your share of calves popping out." Chase laughed. "Let me know if you want to sell any of them."

"Not this round, maybe next time," Luke responded.

"Trying to build up your stock?"

"No, I've already got a buyer for this lot." He didn't elaborate anymore and Chase didn't ask. Still, Tessa wondered who would have made a deal for cattle before they were born.

She was determined to ask Luke, but they got busy, and she forgot.

They had plenty of time to talk on the two-hour drive to Houston and she brought it up.

"So, who's the big spender? Who'd you sell the cattle to?" She leaned on the door of his truck and watched him as she rubbed Lucky, who was curled up in her lap.

"Hmm?" He glanced at her. "Oh, no big spender. Actually, I might even lose money on the first batch."

191

"Batch?" She chuckled. "You make them sound like cookies." She felt her stomach growl and frowned.

"There's this place outside of Tyler, it's called Wild Farms."

She nodded. She'd heard of the place. They were a nature reserve. People paid high dollar to fly in from the city to pretend to be cowboys for a weekend.

"You're selling your cattle to Wild Farms?" When he nodded, she smiled. "So, they aren't going to a slaughter house?"

"God no!" He turned to look at her. "Not my cows. I'm not sure I could do that. It's one thing to buy a burger or a steak, but if I had a hand in their raising and birth... no."

She reached over and took his hand. "I'd have a hard time getting rid of them like that too. You know, when I was in college, I tried to stay away from meat."

He chuckled and squeezed his hand. "How'd that go?"

She shook her head. "I like burgers too much."

"Me too... Speaking of which, how about we stop off at the Brick House. They have some pretty awesome steaks."

"Can't wait..." She sighed and leaned back to enjoy the rest of the drive. "Did you ever imagine

192

that you'd be driving into Houston to record for a major recording studio?"

He laughed. "I never imagined any of this." He glanced at her. "The ranch. The music. The record deal… or you." He took her hand up to his lips and placed a soft kiss across her knuckles. "I guess I'm just lucky."

"Both of us are." She sighed and wondered if her life could get any more perfect.

By the time they made it to their hotel room, the sun had gone down. They were due at the recording studio first thing in the morning, so they locked themselves in their shared hotel room and spent the night watching old television shows and ordering dessert through room service as Lucky curled up between them on the bed.

The next morning, she was so anxious, she threw up. She felt sure she was going to screw everything up, until he took her face in his hands and smiled at her.

"I'm nervous too, but you know what I did to overcome stage fright?"

She shook her head, feeling tears slide down her cheeks.

"I kept my eyes on yours. I focused on making you smile and all my worries disappeared."

Her eyes locked with his and she watched his irises grow. His brown eyes were darker than hers. Her brown eyes were boring. But, his… He had a ring of lighter brown near the outside, and there were so many different hues of brown, gold, and gray that she was almost mesmerized.

"There you go." He talked to her in a low tone, and she relaxed in his arms. "Stay focused on that, and everything else will fall into place."

She nodded and swallowed. "You're right." She closed her eyes and took several deep breaths. "I'm being stupid."

"No, trust me. If it wasn't for you, I'd be in that bathroom, tossing my cookies too."

She laughed. "Is it stupid that I'm not scared to sing in front of a crowd, but recording makes me nervous?"

"No, it makes sense," he said taking her hand and walking out. "Singing in front of a crowd is fleeting, while a recording lasts forever."

He opened the truck door for her and she slid in. "You're right." She felt herself tense again, but he moved closer and kissed her until all the nerves were gone.

"Now, relax. Worse case, it takes more than two weeks to record and we get to spend more time locked in a hotel room together."

He walked around the truck, and she wondered when she should tell him how she felt. If she could make it through the next two weeks, practically living with the man, she was pretty sure she was going to lose her heart and there was nothing and no one who could change that.

When they walked into the studio, her nerves spiked again. Her agent, Charles, introduced them to the band that would be playing along. She tried to remember everyone's names, but she was so nervous that it was hard to keep track.

When they walked into the padded recording room, she reached for Luke's hand and held in a squeal. She'd never imagined being here. She'd dreamed of it, ever since the first song she'd written.

When she looked up at him, his smile soothed her nerves.

"Before we record, Ken has allowed me to use his office so we can sign some papers. Then, if you want, we can give you some time to warm up. But, we'd like to dive right in. I've got your list of songs and wanted to start with "Daylight," if that's okay," he said as they walked away from the studio, down a long hallway. He opened a door with a plaque that read "Kenneth Richie, Comfort Records."

They sat in the office and he went over the paperwork he'd emailed them earlier that week. They'd had Grant look the contract over, and even though this wasn't what he normally dealt with as a lawyer, he was able to explain the contract to them and assured them that it was pretty standard.

Charles would get a ten percent cut. His agency

was paying the cost of the recording, as well as any other up-front expenses. They would start earning a commission once that total was paid back in full.

She didn't care. All she cared about was that people would hear Luke sing her songs.

After signing the papers, they walked back to the studio and Luke sat down with the band members and started warming up.

Of course they would want to start with one of the four songs she was supposed to sing with Luke, with, so she spent a few minutes locked in the sound booth, warming up her voice. Someone delivered a cup of hot tea, which helped.

The red light went on, signaling that they were recording, and all of her nerves disappeared when Luke struck the first chords. Her music flowed around her, and she enjoyed every minute.

They stopped and started almost a dozen times, then took a break for everyone to get something to drink or hit the restroom. They worked until lunch, then enjoyed sandwiches that were delivered.

They worked for several more hours, breaking out each instrument, and having Luke and her sing together, then individually.

After they called it quits for the day, they listened to the rough mix, and she was pleased with how it sounded.

"Once this goes through the full editing process,

it's going to sound amazing," Greg, the producer, said.

"How about some dinner?" one of the guys from the band asked. "We were thinking of hitting Tommy's. It's a seafood place not far from here."

Luke looked over at her and she nodded.

"Sounds good." He took her hand and followed the men outside.

Luke followed the row of cars a few blocks and pulled in beside them.

"If you want to leave, just nudge me," he said before jumping out of the truck to open her door.

Just hearing those words, she felt her heart slip a little more and knew for a fact that she was in love.

Two hours later, she was laughing so hard, she doubted anyone at the large table wanted to leave. She finally could remember everyone's names.

Jeff played drums, Nick was on bass, and Dusty played slide steel guitar. Keith was on the piano.

None of them could stop talking about how much they liked her music.

She'd been nervous when they asked her to play rhythm guitar behind Luke's lead guitar, but she'd enjoyed playing along.

"You know; we've been playing for Comfort Records for a few years now. We've been keeping

197

our eyes out for something we could get behind," Keith broke in after all their plates were removed and another round of beer was delivered. "We talked about it during break." His eyes moved around the table. "If and when you tour, we'd like you to consider taking some of us along."

"Tour?" Luke said, frowning slightly. Then he glanced at her. "I... we hadn't talked..."

"I'm not sure if we're there yet," she broke in.

The men glanced at one another and laughed. "You could easily book a show in every major city now, the way you hit the internet." Jeff shook his head and whistled. "Over a million hits in under a week."

"A million?" she asked, glancing over at Luke.

"Sure," Nick jumped in. "Haven't you kept track?"

"No, we just..." Luke reached for her hand under the table. "We've been kind of busy."

Chapter Fifteen

The next few days flew by so quickly; it was hard to keep track of which day was which. The band had been right about the shocking YouTube numbers, and Grant moved the videos to their YouTube account instead of his and added ads, so they were slowly making money on each video. It wasn't a lot, but seeing the dollars add up was a bonus.

They had finished all four songs with her vocals, and she'd sung backup on a few others. But for the most part, she'd sat in the sound booth and watched Greg push buttons and listened in as everyone did their part. As she listened through the high-tech speakers, she realized how incredible Luke's voice really was.

Lucky had become somewhat of a mascot while they had been there. Everyone loved the dog so much, they took turns walking her and taking her out for breaks. They even hung a picture of the dog in the studio and titled it Lucky Charm.

They spent their days working and their nights curled up to one another. She couldn't have asked for a more perfect time.

They were quickly approaching the end of their time in Houston and only had one last song to work on.

Charles hadn't decided yet which one he liked best, so he asked for a sample of each and was going to let them know in the morning which song he chose. For some reason, this made Tessa very nervous.

Even Luke was wondering why it was taking so long.

"If it was up to me, I'd add them both," he said, running his hand lazily over her bare shoulder.

"I can always write a—"

"Stop," he broke in. It had been a long-standing argument between them. She wanted to write a new, better song, thinking that Charles couldn't decide because he didn't like either of them. Luke believed he loved them both and just couldn't decide. In her heart, she knew that was probably the truth. Still, that didn't stop her from speculating or worrying.

"I bet he picks, 'Follow Me,'" Luke said, causing her to sit up and look down at him.

"Why? Don't you like 'The Fall'?" She loved the way his tan naked body looked against the crisp white hotel sheets. She was actually thinking of replacing her teal sheets with a set of white ones.

"I love 'The Fall.'" I just think 'Follow Me' has more potential for a following. You know, it's easier for fans to sing along with."

"You're right." She rolled onto his chest and looked down at him. "Remember the last time you played at the Rail? I was so shocked to hear that everyone knew the words."

He smiled. "I know. It was fun, though."

She nodded, swallowing the knot in her throat. "Have you thought any more about touring?"

She'd talked to Charles about what it would take to set up a tour and he'd given them the rundown. He had been excited about the possibility, but Luke had put up his hand and told him that he didn't know if he wanted to tour, that he was just asking.

He shook his head slightly and closed his eyes. "I have the ranch to think about." She knew she shouldn't pressure him; it was his decision. She was just backup and the person who had written the songs. He was the star; the one women would be flocking to see.

She felt a little pinch of jealousy in her gut and rolled over to lay next to him, her eyes glued to the ceiling fan.

Over the past two weeks, she'd thought about telling him how she felt so many times, but each time, she'd held her tongue. She wasn't sure if it was fear of rejection or fear of forcing him to repeat those words back to her out of obligation.

After all, if she hadn't asked him to sing, he wouldn't have made a record deal and be here. Did he feel he owed her?

She didn't think she could deal with him feeling obligated to love her in return. Even worse, she didn't think she could handle his rejection.

Finally, several hours later, she fell asleep to the sound of his soft breathing.

The next morning, they stood in the studio and Tessa tried not to pass out. She was sure she would hyperventilate when she saw the woman standing next to Charles.

"Okay, so I had a hard time picking between 'Follow Me' and 'The Fall,' so I had Crystal decide which one she wanted to do as a duet with Luke."

The entire room was silent, and then Crystal Rose walked forward and smiled. "The Fall."

The band members broke out in a cheer.

"You're kidding," Tessa said. "A duet with

202

Crystal Rose?" She blinked a few times. "With Luke?"

"Well, we actually decided to use his full name on the record. But, yes. Lucas James with special guest Crystal Rose, singing 'The Fall,' written by Tessa Keys."

Luke's hand was on her back when her knees buckled.

Tessa had grown up listening to Crystal Rose. The woman had been one of her mother's favorite country singers.

Tears streamed down her face as she was pushed into a chair and handed a glass of water.

"Are you okay, sweetie?" Crystal asked, right next to her.

She couldn't answer through the boulder in her throat so she just nodded, took a drink of water, and closed her eyes. "My mother loved you." She looked up into the woman's blue eyes and felt her heart break.

"'The Fall'… is that about your mother?" she asked.

Again, Tessa nodded. "She died a few months back. Cancer."

"Oh, sweetie. I'm sorry. I lost my mother eight years ago to breast cancer. I know how raw you're feeling now." She smiled slightly. "I promise to do her proud. I just fell in love with the song." She

203

took Tessa's hand and Tessa felt her entire body shake. "You've got a real talent. You know that?" Tessa nodded again. "Your mama would be proud."

That was when Tessa lost it. The tears flowed so fast that even the tissues Luke handed her couldn't dry her eyes.

"I'd be honored," she finally said once her eyes dried a little. "I've always loved hearing you sing."

"If it's okay, Lucas and I wanted to add a dedication before the song?"

Tessa looked to Luke. "We'd like to dedicate it to Leslie Keys and Maya Rose, Crystal's mother." He added.

Tessa smiled and took Crystal's hand. "That's perfect."

For the following two days, she sat in the booth and listened to Luke sing with one of the greatest female country artists of all time. She couldn't count the number of times her body was covered in goosebumps or the boxes of tissue she went through.

When they drove home the next day, she was both exhausted and thrilled. They had promised Charles an answer about touring within a week. He had already promised three full months of touring with several stops in every state in the south.

For some reason, Luke still didn't want to talk to her about it, so she kept avoiding the conversation.

As they drove through town, she couldn't get a handle on how much had changed in her life in the past few months.

"If it's okay with you, I'll drop you off and head home to check on my animals. I'm sure Chase and Grant have been taking good care of them, but I'd like to check up on them anyway. Besides, I think Lucky wants to get home."

She nodded. "I'm going to go in, have a hot bath, then pull on some fresh pajamas and sleep until tomorrow night." She sighed.

He chuckled. "Wish I could join you." He pulled in next to her car. "How about tomorrow night I stop by?"

She sighed. "I'm working at the diner. I have to make up for lost time."

He pulled her close. "How about lunch the following day?"

She nodded. "Sounds good." She leaned over and kissed him. "Night."

Later, as she soaked in the hot water, her mind played over how wonderful everything had been. How meeting Luke had changed her life so much in such a short time.

Then she thought about what her life used to be like and she shivered. Why had she let the opinions of children determine how she felt about herself?

Closing her eyes, she tried to remember the hurtful words the kids used to say to her. None of those words would cause her to even bat an eye now. She was so much stronger. She had so much love in her life. So much friendship. She'd seen so much kindness. Life was worth so much more than words or momentary feelings.

Pulling herself out of the tub, she pulled on her PJs, sat at her desk, and started writing. She was tired of hiding the secret she'd kept for too long. It was time to tell the world why she'd jumped off a bridge.

***

Luke knew Tessa was probably wondering why he'd ditched her, but the truth was, he needed some time alone to think about his future.

They actually wanted him to tour the country. Which meant his name and face would be plastered everywhere… including Austin. No more running or hiding from his past.

He'd always known that someday he'd have to come out of hiding and tell his family and friends where he was, but he'd hoped for a little more time.

He wasn't sure how his family would react to his new career choice. When he pulled up to his house, he sat in the truck for a few minutes. It was about an hour before sunset and he took his time looking around.

The cattle looked happy and fat grazing in the fields and the horses looked content next to them. His little house looked like a slice of heaven. There were still a lot of improvements he wanted to do, but for the most part, there was no place on earth he would rather be... well, maybe in Tessa's arms.

An image of her popped into his head, forcing him to close his eyes. She was beyond anything he'd ever imagined.

His mind flipped and he tried to conjure an image of Kristen, but he just couldn't. All he could remember was feeling pressured. Forced into a life he didn't want. Always doing something someone else wanted. Not having enough time to really decide what he wanted, or who he was.

Well, he was making his own decisions now. He pounded his fist on the steering wheel. And by damn, he wanted to continue singing. If touring was part of it, so be it.

He jumped from the truck, even more determined than when he'd packed up his truck and moved to a small town in the middle-of-nowhere Texas.

He checked on the animals and by the time he made it inside and showered, it was past ten and he didn't want to wake Tessa. He decided to surprise her after work the next night and jumped into bed.

The next day, he caught up on his chores. Then he showered off and dressed in his best pants and dress shirt. He was excited and nervous to tell her, but he'd seen it in her eyes every time she'd tried to talk to him about touring. She wanted it as bad as he did. He'd just let fear rule him. Until now.

He glanced down at his watch and frowned, then headed towards Holly's instead of parking outside Mama's. He'd taken too long in the shower. She had gotten off work almost half an hour ago.

When he parked on the street in front of Holly's and got out, he heard her voice and frowned even more. She was talking to a man. Turning the corner, he saw two dark figures at the base of her stairs.

Chapter Sixteen

$\mathcal{S}$he had forgotten what it was like to be on her feet for eight hours a day. Her back and neck were sore and the arches of both feet were killing her. She had grease and mustard stains on her uniform.

She'd answered all of Mama and Willard's questions about their trip. When she mentioned meeting Crystal, it was like the entire diner stopped. She'd had to repeat the story to the entire dining room. At first it had made the day go by faster, but after she'd told the story half a dozen times, she had a headache and her throat was sore from talking too much.

Luke didn't show up before she clocked out, and she ended up getting a box of chicken fingers

209

and fries to go so she could eat them in the comfort of her own apartment. She'd missed the place, but not as much as she'd thought she would.

There was still a lot she planned on doing, but writing songs was more important. She'd plugged through one last night she'd titled "The Bridge" and planned to write another one tonight. She'd daydreamed about it all during her shift.

She was so excited to dig into it that she didn't realize someone was behind her until she reached the stairs to her apartment. Spinning around, she spotted John Drake a few feet away from her.

"Oh," she gasped, then laughed. "You scared me." She relaxed a little. "I guess I didn't hear you."

"Is it true?" he asked, moving closer to her.

"What?" She hugged the bag of warm food next to her chest.

"That Crystal Rose is singing your songs? That's pretty big time." He stopped less than a foot from her.

"Um, yes, she sang one with Luke." She moved back a step when she realized the foul smell of alcohol was coming from him.

"So, you're kind of a hotshot now." His hand moved out and brushed her hair. She coiled back quickly, and his eyes flashed with anger so quickly that she thought of tossing her food at him and making a run for it.

210

"You think you're too good for me?" he shouted. His hand twisted around and took hold of her neck, squeezing hard until she felt her throat close up. Her entire body froze in fear.

Then, without any notice, a dark shadow flew down the alleyway. A fist came out of nowhere and slammed into John's face, sending his jaw twisting at an odd angle. Blood splattered over her face and his hand released her neck, sending her sprawling back onto the steps.

She landed hard on her butt, half on and half off a step, sending pain shooting up her back. She lost the bag of food somewhere and heard the contents of her purse spill out on the alley floor.

She searched the dark and saw Luke on top of John. Luke had the man pinned down as his fists continued to slam into John's face.

"Stop," she said, but her throat was too raw and no sound came out. She tried again and again until she finally managed to scream. She moved behind Luke and grabbed for his arm. When she touched him, his head turned and his eyes focused on her.

"Are you okay?" He moved quickly and was standing in front of her.

She nodded, since she didn't think her throat could handle talking at the moment.

"Hey!" someone shouted from the mouth of the alley. "What's going on?"

It was Holly. "Someone attacked Tessa. Call the

211

cops," Luke yelled back.

"Oh no! Is she okay?"

"I'm checking. Run in and call the police first. We'll be inside in a minute."

She heard Holly run inside, and less than a minute later, several more people rushed outside. Soon, she was surrounded by people ushering her into the brightness of the coffee shop.

She had a cup of hot tea in her hands and a soft blanket wrapped around her. Luke had stayed outside to watch and make sure John didn't get up and leave.

She was asked so many questions, her head spun. She just shook her head and swallowed the tea. Her throat was on fire and she couldn't control the tears that slid down her cheeks.

She saw the flashing lights outside and worried that Luke would end up in the back of the police car, instead of John.

When she tried to get up to make sure he was okay, she was pushed back down by Holly. "Stay put. Luke is taking care of it. I'm sure Wes or someone will be in shortly."

"But…" she tried to say, but nothing but a squeak came out.

"Shush, I've called Missy over here to check up on you, since I didn't think you'd want to spend any more time in the clinic. Not after all the time you spent there as a kid..."

"What happened to her when she was a kid?" Luke's voice broke the silence of the room.

"Oh." Holly jumped a little. "Um, nothing..." Holly glanced at her and for the first time Tessa realized that her friends had kept her accident from Luke. Which meant... they all knew. They all knew that it hadn't been an accident.

Everyone in town knew she'd tried to kill herself that day so many years ago, and they had cared enough about her that they had kept the knowledge from her.

More tears came out of her eyes and she buried her face in her hands. Then she was picked up gently and carried outside. Instead of heading up the back stairs to her apartment, Luke carried her to his truck and set her gently down in the front seat.

"Here," Holly said. "I packed my last blackberry pie and a carton of ice cream. The cold will help her throat. If it hurts her too much..."

"Yeah," Luke said, nodding. "I'll bring her to the clinic."

Holly reached up and hugged Luke. "Thanks for being there. I don't know what we would have done if anything..."

Luke cleared his throat, stopping Holly.

"Thanks," she repeated.

213

"Anytime. She'll be out at my place."

"When Missy shows up, I can have her stop by there instead?"

"Sounds good." He walked around his truck. Tessa met Holly's eyes and mouthed, "Thank you," to her friend. She was pretty sure Holly understood just what she was thanking her for because tears slid down her face as she nodded and blew a kiss to her.

***

"Is there something you want to tell me?" Luke asked, half an hour after he showed several people out his front door.

It was close to midnight, but he was still so wired, he doubted he could sleep for the next few hours.

Tessa's eyes met his. "I'm not..." Her throat sounded hoarse.

"You don't have to talk just now. Just nod your head if you promise to tell me why you spent a few weeks in the hospital."

She took a deep breath and then nodded.

"Were you sick?" he asked, moving close to her.

She shook her head no and opened her mouth to talk.

"No, just nod or shake your head for now." He handed her a large bowl of ice cream and she

214

chuckled and mouthed, "Too much."

"I'll eat half of it." He sat beside her and pulled her into his arms and reached for the spoon. He scooped a bite and brought it up to her mouth.

"Was it an accident?" Again, she hesitated, then shook her head no. "Okay, you promise to tell me what happened once you get your voice back?" She nodded. "Good, then how about we watch a movie, since we can't talk and I'm still so wired."

She nodded and he reached for the remote. "Do you like scary?" he joked, only to have her nod. "Really?" She nodded again. "Hmmm, how about we settle for comedy?" She looked up and him and cringed. "Really?" She nodded. "Okay, how about sci-fi?" She nodded several times and smiled. "My favorite genre." She reached up and placed a kiss on his lips. Then she took the bowl from his hands and set it aside. She moved up until she was straddling him. Her eyes locked with his.

He was pretty sure she mouthed, "I love you," but he had to blink a few times to make sure.

"What?" His hands dug into her hips. "Did you just…" She nodded. "Um…" He was speechless. "Really?" She nodded again, a smile forming on her lips. Slowly, she mouthed those three words again.

"I…" She pushed her finger over his lips, stopping him as she shook her head.

"Later," she mouthed.

215

With her finger over his mouth, he nodded. Then she leaned down and replaced her finger with her mouth. She tasted sweet and felt like heaven.

He tried to pull away, since his mind was whirling about the fact that she'd just been attacked in an alley, but she was having none of it. She yanked his shirt over his head and reached for his jeans. When her fingers wrapped around him, he jerked off the sofa, taking her with him as he reversed their positions. He pinned her underneath him, kissing her until her legs wrapped around him. She pushed and pulled his jeans down his hips as he popped a couple buttons off her uniform until the dress lay wide open, exposing her silk panty and bra set.

Her skin was pale and so soft looking, he was pretty sure he could never get over the feel of it next to him. He tensed when he saw the large red and purple marks around her throat.

She reached up to cover the marks. "I'm okay," she said and reached for him.

"No, you're not." He tried to pull back, but she locked her legs around his hips and held him in place.

"He could have... If I hadn't shown up..." He closed his eyes to get his anger back under control.

Her fingers ran lightly over his shoulder, causing him to look down at her.

"You were there." She smiled up at him. "By

tomorrow, I'll have my voice back." She tugged on him until he came back down to her. "I'm okay, really." She pressed her lips against his.

"You deserve better. Better than living in a place you have to enter through a back alley." He closed his eyes and took a few deep breaths.

"Luke?" she said softly.

"Yes."

"One thing."

"Anything," he said, looking back down at her.

"Shower," she said and then kissed him. "You, me. Now."

He chuckled, then in one quick motion, picked her up and carried her to the bathroom.

He took his time slowly undressing her and took even longer running his soapy hands over her, enjoying the soft moans that escaped her lips and watching her body react to his touch.

When he slid into her, he knew he loved her too. Actually, he'd probably fallen in love with her before she had with him. He could even pinpoint the exact moment—when he'd stood up on the stage and, by just looking into her eyes, had known peace. Completely.

He wanted to show her more tenderness than he could standing up, she he pulled her from the shower, wrapped a towel around her, and carried her into the bedroom, where he took his time drying her off.

When he laid her on the bed, she sighed and closed her eyes as he ran his mouth and hands over her. He kissed her as he took her slowly until the sunlight broke into the room, showing her how he felt with his body.

Then they lay in each other's arms and slept until he heard pounding on his front door.

Chapter Seventeen

The pounding woke her first. She shook Luke's shoulder and swallowed a few times. She was pretty sure she could manage talking, but didn't want to chance it until she'd had a drink of water.

Luke rolled out of bed and rubbed his hands over his face. "Who the hell could it be at this time?" He glanced over at the clock. She too was surprised to see that it was a quarter past eleven. They had slept most of the day away, curled up tight together after the most magical night in her entire life.

He pulled on his jeans and she decided she might need to get dressed as well. Then she realized her uniform was probably lying on his living room floor. She searched his drawers as he walked out to answer the front door. She found a pair of his sweats and a black T-shirt to pull on. Still barefoot, she walked into the bathroom to run his brush through her hair.

When she walked out into his living room, it was to yelling. Not his, but a woman's. A man and woman stood just inside his doorway, their arms crossed over their chests. The woman had been yelling, but stopped dead when she stepped out of the bedroom. Instantly, Tessa wished she'd stayed in the room.

"Who the hell is this?" the woman asked.

Luke's head spun around. Tessa could see the pain and anger in his eyes and wanted to rush to his side, but something in his eyes told her he couldn't handle it at the moment.

She took a step back and came up hard against his bedroom door.

"Mom, Dad, this is Tessa." He walked over and took her hand. "She was attacked last night, so she probably doesn't have a voice right now."

"I…" She tried to speak, but it came out raspy.

"Is she the reason you ran away?" his mother accused.

"Ran away?" Tessa asked. It came out as a chuckle. Luke was a full-grown man but his mother seemed to think of him like a child.

"Does she know about Kristen?"

Tessa felt her heart skip. Kristen? Who? She dropped her hand from his. The fact that he didn't pull it back into his hand scared her.

"No, no one here does." His eyes moved to the floor.

"Why would you do this to us?" His mother moved over and touched him on the shoulder.

"I… I needed a fresh start. Away from the pain and the guilt."

"Luke?" Tessa heard herself say his name, but her head was spinning and she wasn't sure it was her that actually spoke.

"So, you're sleeping with some stranger that knows nothing about your fiancée?"

Tessa took a step back then. She turned and walked into the living room and without a word, pulled on her shoes. She could hear Luke arguing with his parents, but didn't care. She no longer heard a word he said. Instead, the word fiancée played over and over in her mind.

Luke had run away from his fiancée. He'd left a woman at the altar. So? Maybe he'd needed a fresh start like he'd said. Maybe he didn't really love the woman, Kristen. Maybe this was the life he wanted.

After pulling on her shoes, she walked back towards the front door.

"I… I'm going to go," she said. "I called my dad to pick me up."

"Tessa." Luke took her shoulders in his hands. "I'm sorry about all this. I'd like to explain."

She nodded. "Later." Her eyes moved over to where his parents stood.

She didn't spare them a word. She walked outside to wait for her dad, praying that he would hurry up.

***

Luke's back teeth were grinding when he heard his front door shut. Every ounce of him wanted to rush after Tessa, but his parents stood between him and the doorway. He knew they wouldn't allow him to leave without explaining to them first.

"Why don't you come in?" he said, turning towards the kitchen, not really caring if they followed him into the house or not. He flipped on the coffee pot, then walked back to his room to pull on a shirt.

By the time he came back into the kitchen, his folks had made themselves at home. Well, as much as they could in a place he could clearly tell was way beneath them.

"Why are you here?" he asked. "How did you find me?"

"Well, I would think it was rather easy for anyone to find you nowadays. All they would have to do is open the web browser." His mother sighed. "Really!" She shook her head. "How embarrassing. Do you know, Judy and Larry came over for dinner last week and sprung the whole thing on us? We looked like fools, not knowing what they were talking about."

"You could have called. We were worried about you," his father added.

"Robert." His mother glared across the table at his father. "That's not the point. You should have called. We had no idea where you had disappeared to. Or what you were doing. Everyone asked about you and we couldn't even tell them what had happened to you." She took a sip of the coffee he'd placed in front of her. "We showed up to your place, and it was empty. Then we found out from Carl that you'd cashed out some of your stocks." She set the mug down a little too hard and coffee spilled onto his table.

"I bought this place with *my* money." He made sure to emphasize the word.

"Lucas, why on earth would you want to live here?" His mother glanced around, clearly appalled at everything she saw. "This is some kind of joke. Right?"

"No, mother. I'm staying here. I'm fixing this place up. I've started a music career. I've signed contracts and I'm planning to go on tour... and I want to be with Tessa."

223

The room was silent for a while.

"You've had your laugh, Lucas." His mother stood up, followed more slowly by his father. "We'll deal with all this mess later. Go pack your stuff and we'll head out. I'm sure everyone will be happy that you're back." She turned to go, but his father's hand on her shoulder stopped him.

"Clarissa, I'm not sure he's going to just fall in line anymore," his father said. "He's a grown man. Look around. He's made something for himself here. For his life." His father turned his mother towards him. "Look into his eyes. He's happy. Isn't that what we always wanted for him?"

His mother's blue eyes met his. Her breath hitched several times. "I... I can't let you go. We almost lost you before and I don't think I could bear it if you left again."

He walked over and wrapped his arms around her frail frame. "I'm not going anywhere. I've found my home. The place I want to be. I may go on tour, but I plan on coming back here. Being here. Always."

"I'm not moving to some podunk town." She stomped her foot. "I refuse to live like a... hillbilly."

Luke laughed. "I'm not asking you to. I'm staying. You're going home to Austin."

"But... It's..."

"Only four hours away," he added. "Not a

million."

"That's too far." Her hands came up and brushed the stubble on his face. "You've been gone too long."

His eyebrows shot up. "You aren't mad at me?"

"Yes, I'm livid."

"About the accident?"

She frowned. "Why would we be mad about the accident?"

"We were fighting." His eyes flew to the floor.

"So?" his father added in. "That doesn't affect the truck driver that ran the red light. Or the fact that Kristen was driving and couldn't react in time."

"If I had…"

His mother's hands on his face stopped him. She jerked his head up until his eyes met hers.

"There was nothing you could have done." He watched tears roll down her face. "Nothing. We could have just as easily lost you that day. There isn't a day that goes by that I don't feel guilty for feeling glad that it was Kristen instead of you."

His throat closed up. "I…" He shook his head. "I cheated on her. I had called off the wedding."

"That doesn't matter anymore." His father walked over and put a hand on his arm. "What matters now is what you do with your life. Are you

225

happy here?"

Luke nodded. "Very."

"Do you love the girl?" his father asked.

"Tessa."

"Do you love Tessa?"

"Yes," he answered quickly.

"Then I see no reason to dwell on the past." He turned to his wife. "Do you?"

Luke's mother shook her head. "We never wanted that for you. We only wanted what was best for you." She wiped a tear from her eyes. "But we had hoped your happiness would be closer to us." She chuckled.

Luke walked over and wrapped her once more in his arms. She cried against his chest as his father shook his head and rolled his eyes. "Women," he mouthed, causing Luke to chuckle.

"Now, if you're done soaking our son's shirt, maybe we can have some lunch? I'm starved, since you made me drive straight through this morning."

He spent the rest of the day with his folks. He hadn't had time to set up a guest room yet, so he settled them in his room after a quick change of sheets and headed into town to find Tessa.

He assumed she would be at work, but when he showed up at Mama's, Jamella told him she'd taken the week off to recover.

He instantly began to worry about her. Why had he let her walk out the door without making sure she was okay?

When he pounded on her apartment door, April rushed from the coffee shop and yelled up to him, "She's not there."

"Where is she?"

"I think she's staying with her dad." She tilted her head. "Thank you for saving her, by the way." The woman smiled up at him. "We're all keeping an extra eye on her, and Savannah had Billy install a security light and camera." She nodded to the new hardware above the stairs. "We have a monitor behind the bar now and can watch who comes and goes from there."

"Good," he said, before getting into his truck. If he needed to knock on every door in town, he was going to find her tonight.

His father said she'd taken a walk, so he drove around the town, slowly, trying to find her. When he spotted Savannah at Mama's, he stopped and asked if she'd seen her.

"You might want to check the bridge on McKinney Street."

"Why?"

"We used to meet there every day. That's where…"—she shook her head and shivered—"she almost died."

227

Those words played over and over in his head as he drove the mile and half to the cement bridge.

He pulled into the dirt before the bridge and saw her leaning against the high cement wall. She looked sad. Like her heart had been broken. He realized he was the one who had broken it.

If he wanted any chance at happiness, he would have to confess everything to her.

Chapter Eighteen

They've changed so much about this place, Tessa thought as she leaned against the thick cement wall.

Gone was the old covered bridge with its charm and its rotted wood planks. After her "accident," the town had demolished that old thing, and the state had come in months later and built a sturdy cement bridge that was very practical, safe, and boring.

She sighed as she watched the water flow slowly below her. How many times had she sat, her feet dangling above the water, dreaming, crying?

She must have spent as much time on this bridge as she had in Mr. Walker's field with

Speedy.

She'd asked for the rest of the week off from Mama's because she didn't think she could deal with all the questions. Not to mention the hurt. Her mind was playing over the scene at Luke's house.

She'd believed they'd made progress. Yet, she was still hiding something from him, just like he'd hidden something major from her.

So, he'd broken off an engagement. Who cares? She'd only tried to kill herself and nearly succeeded. And now it appeared that everyone in town had known about it all these years and no one had said a word to her. They had all kept her secret.

Her heart had sunk when she'd realized that her mother must have known before she'd died that she had actually jumped instead of fallen. She didn't think she could deal with that knowledge.

She had worked up enough courage to ask her father, and he'd nodded his head as his eyes teared up.

"The investigator said the hole in the wood was too small for you to fall through." He'd wiped his eyes on his handkerchief. "We figured you'd tell us when you wanted. Even though you'd left the note, everyone had assumed... Besides, everyone knew you'd changed... after."

She'd nodded. "It changed me." She'd taken his other handkerchief from him and used it.

It had. She'd changed because of the good people in Fairplay and because of Luke. She didn't know what his plans were. She figured he'd held off from touring because of his fiancée. He'd held off from making a decision about his future because he wasn't sure if he was going to stay in Fairplay.

It was funny, she'd come back into town pretty sure that it was just a stop and now she couldn't imagine herself living anywhere else. Luke had acted all along like he was determined to stay in town, but held off from making that commitment, other than buying a place. She realized that all along, he'd never really committed to the town, to the people.

As she looked down over the water, she wondered how her life would change if he decided to go back to Austin, or wherever he'd come from. Back to his family. To his fiancée.

She straightened her shoulders and took a deep breath. She would be heartbroken, but not broken.

Just then she heard a truck. She held her breath when she noticed it was Luke's and watched as he pulled over to park on the side of the road.

When he walked over to her it was almost too dark to see the emotions in his eyes.

"Isn't this dangerous?" He glanced around. "Standing on the bridge. There's not even a sidewalk."

"Not really." She turned and leaned against the railing. "There's only half a dozen homes up that way." She nodded up the hill. "And most of them exit the highway instead of using this bridge."

"I worked things out with my folks. They're no longer freaking out."

She chuckled. "Parents are good for freaking out." She turned back around and watched as the sun sank lower in the sky.

"I'm sorry I didn't tell you about Kristen before." He said. She shrugged and closed her eyes. "I felt guilty."

"For breaking it off?"

He shook his head. "We were fighting. I'd just returned from a four-month tour overseas and she had picked me up from the airport." He leaned on the cement. "She was driving back to my apartment." He closed his eyes and she watched his face. "She was yelling at me since I wanted to call off the wedding. She was determined to get married because she was pregnant."

"Oh." She felt her heart skip.

"Two months pregnant."

"Oh." Anger spread into her quickly.

"She begged me. If I didn't claim the baby as mine, her parents would disown her. She was trying to convince me to tell everyone that it was mine. And when it came two months early, we would explain that she'd had it early."

"What did you do?" she asked, reaching out to touch his hand.

"I don't know what I would have done. I remember it in slow motion. She turned her head towards me. Her blue eyes focused on me, the word *please* escaped her lips, and a cement truck ran the light and t-boned us."

His eyes closed and a tear slipped down his cheek. She didn't know what to say or do. So she waited. When his eyes opened again, he looked down at the water. "I remember hitting my head and seeing a bright light. I woke the next day." He shook his head. "A couple broken bones, some cuts, but... Kristen was gone. I never told anyone about the baby." He turned to her. "No one ever found out."

"Luke." She walked to him and wrapped her arms around him.

He pulled back and looked at her. "A few days later I checked myself out of the hospital, cashed out some stock options from my family's business, hopped in my truck, and drove until I stopped. Here." He glanced around. "The first place that called to me. And I have no plans of ever leaving." He wrapped his arms around her.

"I have a secret too." She pulled away and stepped closer to the edge. "I was a pretty scary kid. I was wiry, my hair was stringy, and I had braces. Braces with a mouth guard that went around my head." She cringed at the memory. "They put it on me when I was in third grade."

She heard him make an "ouch" noise, but didn't turn around.

"Needless to say, I was picked on... a lot. Which led to your basic teenage depression. My parents didn't understand, since they were so much older. The teasing and bullying grew worse. I don't even know where to begin. Imagine what you stopped in the alley, but add the entire football team there instead. There wasn't anyone to stop it or to stand up for me. Sometimes, it was the cheerleaders doing the kicking and pushing."

He walked over and wrapped his arms around her.

"I'm sorry." He placed a kiss on the top of her head and she melted back into him.

"By the time I was fifteen, I'd already started cutting myself." She turned over her arms and showed him the light scars that you could only see if you looked really close. "Then, I would come here." She looked around. "Before they built the new bridge, I would sit on the edge, dangle my feet over, and dream about just leaning forward."

She felt him tense and closed her eyes.

"Savannah stopped me one day. I heard her coming... she was walking her daughter. I had written my parents a letter and had planned on it being that day. But she talked to me." Her throat closed up and her breath hitched. "She never understood what that meant to me. How much a simple conversation could mean to a girl who had never had a friend. She made me promise to come again the next night and then the next. It seemed to help for a while. I felt the depression slipping to the back of my mind, but then I decided to change myself like she suggested. 'If you don't like what you see in the mirror, change it.' It sounded simple." She sighed and opened her eyes.

Luke's arms were wrapped tight around her. She knew he was waiting for her to continue.

"I went to the Grocery Stop and bought a box of hair dye and a few girl magazines. I pulled my mother's good scissors out and tried my best to make myself look like the girls in the pictures. I even convinced my mother to let me go clothes shopping in Tyler. Of course, we didn't have a lot of money, so I was limited. And, to be honest, I had no sense of style. The next day when I went to school, I was pretty proud of my new look."

She took a step out of his arms and crossed her arms over her chest, missing his warmth. But she needed to stand on her own.

"What happened?" he asked, moving beside her.

She closed her eyes and took a deep breath. "Let's just say, I ran home in the rain, more determined than ever to stop the pain. I pulled the very vague note I'd written months before out and laid it on my pillow. Then, I walked here, to the bridge and didn't even hesitate." He reached for her, but she jerked away. "I'm broken." She didn't mean for it to come out so loud.

"No, Tracy was broken. Theresa was a child her parent's always dreamed of having. Tessa is the strongest woman I've ever known." He walked to her and this time, when he gathered her up in his arms, she went willingly.

"What happened next?" he asked after a moment of silence.

"I... I crawled out of the water. It was winter. The water level was pretty low, so when I hit the water, I hit the bottom. I remember hearing my leg shatter under water." She shivered. "When I first tried to pull myself out, I slipped and broke my arm on a rock." She glanced over at her arm and remembered the pain. "I was in so much pain... I freaked. At that moment, I realized that nothing was as bad as the pain. So, I crawled out of the water. Soaked, freezing, broken. I cried until my eyes were dry and my mind was clear. I lay there and watched the stars overhead. I was in and out of consciousness. My parents went to the cops, who couldn't officially report me missing for twenty-four hours. By the next morning, my mother had gone to Savannah's and then they came here. Billy found me, there." She nodded and pointed to the side of the river. It was too dark now to see clearly, but the memory of that bank would be imbedded in her mind for the rest of her life. "They saved me."

"No," he broke in. "You saved yourself."

She looked up at him and smiled. "You saved me, too."

***

"Me?" There was no way he could explain how much it meant to him that she'd opened up to him. What it did to him to hear the pain and sorrow she'd gone through as a child. The way he'd reacted to the events of the last year of his life seemed childish now that he'd heard what she'd gone through. "How have I saved you?"

She smiled. "I wasn't going to stay in Fairplay."

"Everyone knew that," he joked and she shook her head.

"I would have probably spent years roaming around, not knowing where I belonged. Because of you, I'm home." She leaned up and kissed him.

"You're the one who saved me." When she shook her head, he stopped her. "I was running from the pain. I'd pretty much talked myself into never being happy again. The guilt I'd felt, holding it all in…" He closed his eyes and rested his head on hers. "It was too deep."

She nodded and wrapped her arms around him.

"Because of you, I've found what I was made for." He looked into her brown eyes and wished more than anything that he could see clearly. The moonlight and stars were not bright enough to shine on her face.

He took her hand in his and started moving.

"Luke?" She chuckled. "What are you doing?"

"Dancing with the woman I love." He leaned down and kissed her. "The one I want to be with for the rest of my life. The one who will hold my child in her arms, cradle our love in her heart." He hadn't realized he was singing, until a tear fell down her face. "You'll hold my hand; you'll take my heart with every kiss. Our love with grow; it will spread to the stars. We'll always be together; and never apart." He whispered the last next to her ear. "I love you, Tessa. Say you will marry me."

He felt her chest heave and pulled back. Her eyes were wet and she had a huge smile on her lips. "I only wish I had the right words to sing back to you. Something half as beautiful as what you've given me."

"You do… All you have to do is say yes."

"Yes," she said as they danced under the stars on the very bridge where the old her had died.

Epilogue

Tessa stood back and watched the yard full of kids and laughed. She'd changed from her mother's cream-colored wedding dress, which she'd had altered slightly to fit her taller frame. She was wearing a sundress covered in flowers and had her red boots on underneath. Most of the other wedding guests were dressed casually as well.

Deciding to have a true country wedding was the best decision she'd made. Well, besides marrying the sexiest cowboy alive. At least that's what the magazines were calling him.

Their album had hit the shelves and had quickly topped all the charts. They were heading out to tour together in less than three weeks, which meant a very short honeymoon. She didn't mind; they were looking at the tour as part of their honeymoon. Especially since she'd never been to most of the places they were booked at.

"How's my wife?" Luke came up behind her and wrapped his arms around her waist.

"Perfect." She took a deep breath. "Nothing could make this day better." She felt her heart skip. "Well…"

"Your mother?" he asked.

She nodded. "I miss her."

"I wish I could have gotten to know her." He

239

turned her around and kissed her softly.

"It's funny. If she hadn't been sick, I wouldn't have come home. And we wouldn't have met. So, in a way, because of her, I have you." She sighed.

"Bittersweet?"

"Yeah,"

"Well, everyone was wondering when we're going to ride off into the sunset." He smiled and turned as Tex and Speedy walked towards them.

The two horses had white flowers braided into their manes and tails. Their saddles had lace and ribbons tied to them.

She frowned and then laughed when she heard clanking and leaned over to see several empty beer cans trailing behind them.

"What have you done to my horse?"

"Me?" He laughed. "Talk to Savannah and Alex. I think even Haley had a hand in this."

She smiled. "My friends." She shook her head.

"What?" He pulled her closer.

"Nothing, I was just thinking that saying my friends sounds almost as good as saying my husband."

He kissed her until the cheers broke them apart. "Well?" He smiled down at her. "How about riding away with me into the sunset and living happily ever after?"

She took a deep breath. "That sounds perfect."

He helped her up on her horse, then jumped up on the back of Tex. When he held out his hand for hers, she took it without hesitation.

"Shall we, Mrs. James?" He smiled over at her.

"Yes, I think we shall." She kicked lightly and sent the horses across the field towards the setting sun and a new chapter of her life. She knew it was going to be nothing but wonderful.

THE END

Finding Pride - *Chapter One*

*A*s the sun disappeared behind a dark cloud, a white sedan crept slowly down the winding road. A wall of trees on either side gave the impression that the only way out was to forge ahead. The black pavement weaved around tight bends, up and down rolling hills. If you could witness the scene from above, it would appear similar to a white mouse running through a maze on its way to find some cheese.

Several minutes had passed since the last open field. Every now and then a quick glance of a farmhouse or a barn would appear. But for now, the only view was the gray of the sky, the green of the trees, and the dark surface of the road.

The car was traveling towards freedom that had come at the worst price: death. Megan Kimble had just lost the last of her family.

Hours later, the sun peeked out of the clouds, landing on the small crowd gathered around a casket. Mist and fog hung in the afternoon air. The sun's rays made the hill overlooking the small town of Pride, Oregon, appear to be cut off from civilization, like an island floating in a sea of fog. Not a sound came from the gathered mourners. Each person stood with their head down, looking at the dark, wet wood of the casket.

Megan stood in front of the crowd dressed in a dark skirt and a black raincoat. She looked down as tears silently rolled down her cheeks. Her long blonde hair was neatly tied back with a clip. The right sleeve of her coat hung empty, and her arm was tucked close to her body, encased in a white cast from her upper arm to just above her wrist.

Looking up, she gazed around the cemetery, not really noticing the people, only the old and crumbled headstones. Her eyes paused on a tall figure in the distance that appeared to hover above the mist. Blinking a few times to clear the moisture from her eyes, she realized it was a huge headstone in the shape of an angel with arms outstretched towards the heavens. It seemed to be reaching up in desperation, in need of a helping hand to ascend above.

Her thoughts drifted to Matt, and she looked back down at the casket. He had always called her his little angel. Looking at the simple wooden casket through teary eyes, she remembered her brother's face as it looked fifteen years ago when she had awakened in a hospital bed with her young body covered in bruises, the memories of violence by her father's hand gone, along with their parents' lives.

Matt's was the first face she had seen in the cold sterile room. His face had been streaked with tears, his eyes red as he'd comforted her. "Little

Meg, everything will be okay. I'll take care of you now. Don't worry my little angel."

Her thoughts snapped back to the cemetery as they lowered the casket into the wet ground. What had she ever done to deserve such a great brother? What had she ever given back to him? He'd given up everything for her, yet she couldn't think of one thing she'd given him except lies.

Feeling hopeless and isolated, she began to wonder what she had left to live for. Why continue? She was all alone now; there was no one left to share her life with. Realizing it was probably Derek's influence causing her dark thoughts, she tensed. Lifting her head, she tried to dismiss the thoughts of her ex-husband. He didn't matter anymore, she told herself. He was out of her life forever.

As she stood in the old cemetery surrounded by a hundred strangers, she felt utterly alone. Matt had been her family, the only family that had really mattered. She had an aunt somewhere, but she hadn't seen or heard from the woman in over fifteen years.

Glancing over, she noticed the priest walking towards her and quickly wiped the tears from her face. He was a short, stout man who was dressed in long, black robes. He wore a wide-brimmed hat that covered his curly silver hair. His face seemed gentle and kind. She could see that his eyes were red from his own tears. He had been very generous in the words he'd spoken about her brother during the short service.

She wasn't Catholic. Neither was her brother, but at this point she wasn't going to object. It had been a wonderful service and so many people had turned out. She didn't know who had organized the service, but she was sure that the priest had had a big hand in it.

"Hello, dear, I'm Father Michael. We spoke on the phone a few days ago," he said, as he took her by the hand. His hands were warm and comforting. "Matt was such a nice young man. I'll miss him dearly."

"Thank you. I'm sorry I wasn't able to get here sooner. I would have helped you plan his service—"

"Don't mention it. We all pitched in to help. That's the wonderful thing about small towns." He smiled and patted her hand a little. "The people in Pride don't usually take to strangers, but Matt just fit in. He became part of the family, you might say. I know he wasn't Catholic, but he did enjoy a good sermon and always attended our social events. Your brother was very well liked around here."

It didn't sound like he was talking about her brother. Matt had always been somewhat of a loner and had never really taken to crowds. But then again, they'd grown apart from each other when he'd moved out west to Oregon.

As the priest continued talking to her about Matt and the town of Pride, she looked around at the crowd of strangers in the muddy cemetery. It appeared that the whole town had braved the wet weather for her brother's funeral. There were numerous faces, both young and old, many weatherworn from years on local fishing boats. She was used to being in crowds, having lived in a large city most of her life, but now it felt like every set of eyes were on her.

Shaking her head clear and taking another look around, she could see that, in fact, almost no one was looking directly at her. As her eyes scanned around, something else caught her gaze. A pair of the lightest silver-blue eyes she'd ever seen looked back at her through the crowd. The man stood a head taller than everyone else around him, and he was staring directly at her. For a moment, she forgot everything, including blinking.

The man had dark brown wavy hair, which was a little long and reached over his coat collar. From what she could see of him under his leather coat, he appeared to be thin. His face could have easily been etched in marble and put on display. His jaw was strong with the smallest of clefts in his chin. His lips were full and his nose was straight, but it was his eyes that caught her attention again. He was staring at her like he wanted to say something to her from across the crowded cemetery.

When Father Michael stepped between them, he broke the trance she'd been in. Blinking, she tried to refocus on the short priest. He was attempting to encourage her to stop by the church for services sometime.

"Megan, I feel like you're already part of the flock. I'm sure we'll be seeing you next week. If there is anything we can do for you, just let me know," the father said while patting her hand. "You will let us know if you need any help moving in, what with your hurt arm and all."

She looked down at her right arm enclosed in the white cast. She had it tucked closely under her raincoat, which she had left unzipped. The pain was a dull throb now, but that didn't make the terrible memories go away.

"The Jordan's are your nearest neighbors. They were very good friends of Matt's. The two boys are young and strong. I'm sure they'll be glad to come down and help you move in your things." There was a matchmaking look in the man's eyes, and she tried to take a step backwards, but her hand was still engulfed by his larger one. "And I'm sure their sister is looking forward to getting them out of her hair for a few hours," he said with a wink.

"Thank you, Father. I'll try to stop by the church for services. I don't have much to move in, only a few bags, but thank you for offering." It was the truth. Megan had sold what little furniture she had left. In fact, she'd been living out of her suitcase for the past few weeks.

"Well, now, if you change your mind, let me

know," he said, patting her hand one more time.

Just then a large woman walked up to them. She had on a very bright blue dress covered in white flowers. Over it, she had a slick black raincoat that covered only half of the dress and half of the woman. She reminded Megan of a peacock all dressed up with its feathers ruffled.

"Father Michael, you let go of that girl's hand so I can shake it. It's a great pleasure to finally meet you, Megan," the woman said while shaking her hand with a firm, warm grip. "I'm Patty O'Neil. I run the local grocery store. I've heard lots about you from your dear departed brother, God bless him." The woman quickly crossed herself and continued. "I'm sure proud to finally meet you. O'Neil's Grocery. It's right down on Main Street. You can't miss it," she said. "It's been in my family for generations. Well, if there is anything we can do…" She trailed off as the next person approached her.

And so it went, the entire town shaking her hand and offering their help in any manner possible.

Todd Jordan silently watched Matt's younger sister. He'd recognized her instantly from the picture Matt had kept on his desk. She was a lot thinner now and very pale. She looked lost. Her broken arm, which she held against her tiny body, made her look even more so. He'd scanned her from head to toe when she'd arrived at the cemetery. The raincoat she wore reached halfway down her slender body, and her heels looked very sensible as they sat halfway sunk in the mud.

He remembered Matt telling him that she was recently divorced but couldn't remember any more details. All he knew was that his friend hadn't been happy about the circumstances. His thoughts were interrupted when Father Michael approached him.

"Well, now, young Todd." The father always called him "young" even though he was now in his mid-thirties. "It's a shame, yes, sir. Her heart is broken. It is your duty as Matt's best friend to make sure you and your family help her settle in. Such a lovely thing, too. To think she'll be living in that old, drafty house all by herself." The father shook his head.

Matt's house wasn't drafty. If anything, it was in better shape than his own. He could tell the good father was probably up to his old matchmaking schemes.

"And to think, the poor girl will be moving in all by herself, and in the state she's in, too. She could hardly shake my hand." Here it comes, he thought, as his gaze once again swept over to where the object of their conversation stood. She was now surrounded by half the town and looked very lost.

"You need to do the right thing by Matt and make sure his little sister gets settled in safely. God has some answers for her. She's come halfway across the world all alone to bury her poor brother." Father Michael shook his head. "I want you to promise me that you and your family will stop by the house often, you hear me?" he said with a sad look on his face.

Todd's gaze swept back to the priest. He knew that look. It was the same look he and a friend had gotten in high school after sneaking in to the cemetery with the Blake girls to try to scare them on Halloween night. The father had tried to scold them, but the entire time, he had been laughing at them, instead.

"Yes, Father," he murmured. Father Michael nodded his head and turned away to greet another group of people.

Todd looked back over at Megan and saw that she was even paler than before. He grabbed his sister's arm as she was walking past him and nodded in Megan's direction.

"Someone needs to go save her," he said under his breath.

"What do you suggest I do?" Lacey said with a stern look, placing both hands on her small hips.

"I don't know. You're the one who's good at breaking things...up," he added after his sister's eyes heated. Then he grabbed her shoulders and pointed her in Megan's direction.

He saw Lacey's shoulders slump a little after taking in the sight of Megan being swamped by the whole of Pride.

"Humph," Lacey grunted and started marching towards the growing crowd. His sister may be small, but she packed the biggest punch in town.

Megan stood there as an older gentleman talked to her. She hadn't caught his name when he'd barged to the front of the line and grabbed her hand.

"I didn't know Matt all that well, but he was a nice young man. He always had wonderful things to say about my bar, never once starting a brawl. Broke a couple up, though," the bar owner said with a crooked grin. "Always such a nice m-m-m," he stuttered.

Concerned, she quickly looked up from the man's hand, which was tightly gripping her own. Standing beside the bar owner was a pixie. Megan didn't believe in fairy tales, but there was no other way to describe the woman. Megan had a strong urge to walk around the petite creature and see if wings were tucked under her dark purple raincoat. The woman was perfect, from the tip of her pixie-cut black hair to the toes of her green galoshes. Galoshes, Megan noted, that didn't have a speck of dirt on them. She was shorter than Megan and very petite with rounder curves. Her skin was fair and her eyes were a crystal gray blue. She had a cute nose that turned up slightly at the end and full lips that were a light shade of pink. She also had a commanding look on her face.

The bar owner literally backed away without even finishing his sentence, then he quickly walked away without so much as a glance back. Within seconds, everyone who'd gathered around her had wandered off, all without a single word from the pixie.

"How...?" Megan's voice squeaked, so she cleared her throat and started again, "How did you do that?"

"Well, it takes years of practice," the pixie said with a smile. "I'm Lacey Jordan." Her voice was smoky and laced with sexuality. "I was very good friends with your brother. I'm sorry he's gone."

The simple words touched something inside Megan. She could tell there was truth behind them. Lacey reached over and lightly grabbed Megan's good arm and then led her towards a row of parked cars.

"I'm also your neighbor. Shall we get you in out of the weather and home where you belong? We've made some meat pie for dinner, and I'm sure by the time we get there, the whole town will be right behind us. We'll go get my brothers and take you home."

"Oh, please, I don't want to be a bother. I'll be fine." Megan felt compelled to follow the small woman who still had a light hold on her arm and an air of command that surrounded her.

"Nonsense! It's no bother at all. Plus, if you turn down dinner," she said with a slight smile, "my brother Iian might get his feelings hurt. It's not every day he makes the family's famous dish." She continued walking towards the row of cars. "Come on then, let's get you out of this rain."

Megan looked up at the skies and at that exact moment, it started to lightly rain. Her mouth fell open in shock, but when a big fat drop landed on her bottom lip, she quickly closed it. Lacey was still lightly holding her arm and pulling her towards the parked cars near the side of the small white church.

Having not eaten before her flight to Portland, Megan felt her stomach growl. Exhaustion was settling in, and she felt a chill come over her bones. She wasn't sure what meat pie was, but if it had meat in it, she knew she could tolerate it.

"Oh! I'm sorry." She stopped walking, and Lacey turned and looked at her. "I forgot to mention that I have a rental car over there." She pointed slightly with her injured arm towards a small white sedan that she'd hastily rented at the airport four hours earlier.

"Give me the keys and my brothers can drive it over to the house for you," Lacey said, waving towards a man who had the same rich black hair. He'd been standing towards the back of the buildings in the shadows, so far back that Megan hadn't even noticed he was there.

As he stepped out, she saw that his hair was longer than his sister's. The man strolled over, appearing to be in no hurry, and he looked like he rather enjoyed the nasty weather and his surroundings. To say that he was tall would be an understatement; he must have been six and half feet and it only took him a couple of strides to reach where they stood.

Megan had to crane her neck to look up into his face, and she noticed that he had the same light eyes as his sister. His chin was strong with a tiny cleft, and his lips held a lazy smile that made him look rather harmless. Lacey handed him the keys to the rental car, then waved her hands in a sequence of patterns in front of her.

Lacey turned back to her. "Megan, this is my brother Iian. He's hearing impaired and uses sign language to communicate, but he can also read lips really well," she said while continuing to sign. Then turning her face away from his she said, "He likes to eavesdrop, so be careful what you say while facing him."

Smiling, Megan turned back to Iian in time to see the quick flash of humor in his eyes as he signed something to his sister. She gestured something back to him and hit him on the shoulder in a sisterly way.

"Come on, Megan. Iian will take care of your car." They began walking towards the cars as the rain came down harder. Groups of people without umbrellas were quickly sprinting to their vehicles. Others with umbrellas were making their way more slowly.

When Megan sank into the passenger seat of Lacey's sedan, chills ran up and down her spine. Lacey got in behind the wheel and started the engine. She turned the heater on full blast, and as it started to warm the inside of the car, Megan felt she could happily fall asleep right there.

They pulled away from the small church and the now-empty cemetery. The windshield wipers were clearing the rain from her view with a soft squeak, but Megan still felt like she wasn't able to see much beyond the path that the headlights were cutting through the fog. Then she sat up a little straighter and looked over at Lacey, who had her eyes on the road. Realizing she had just gotten into a stranger's car, she tensed. What did she really know about this small woman?

"You don't need to worry," Lacey said, not taking her eyes off the road. "I'm not going to kidnap you." She turned her head slightly and smiled. "We'll deliver you to your brother's house before everyone else gets there. I hope you don't mind, but we invited a few close friends over for potluck. It's what Matt would have wanted, something small. Your brother was very well liked around town, and people will want to bid him goodbye in this manner." She smiled sadly.

"Of course." She relaxed a little and rested her head against the window, enjoying the soft hum of the engine and the gentle beat of the wipers. By the time they pulled off the main road, the sky was dark; the sun hadn't come back out before setting for the night.

"Here we are now." Lacey parked the car so the headlights hit the house full force. "Matt spent most of the first year remodeling the place. I think you'll like what he's done with it." Lacey smiled at her.

Looking through the car window, Megan saw a large, white two-story house. Long green shutters sat on either side of picture windows that lined the whole front of the house. The front door was bright red with a brass knocker, and there were stained-glass windows on either side of the door. The windows seemed to glow brightly in the night.

Following Lacey's lead, she opened her door, and together they raced for the front porch through the light rain. Standing on the huge, brightly lit covered porch, she watched Lacey open the front door with a key from her own key chain. As they crossed the threshold, Megan's rental car pulled up in the driveway and parked next to Lacey's sedan.

Watching from the doorway, she saw Iian step out of the car along with the silver-blue-eyed man she had seen in the cemetery. Both men looked up to the front door and nodded to her and then stepped behind the rental car and started pulling her overnight bags from the trunk.

"They'll get those. Come on inside out of the cold," Lacey said. She walked towards the back of the house, leaving Megan standing alone in her brother's doorway.

Even though her brother had lived here for several years, she'd never visited Oregon before today. There had always been a reason not to visit him. Looking down at the cast on her arm, she realized that this was the reason she'd put off the last visit. The broken arm had been one more thing she had hidden from her brother, and she wished that she hadn't postponed that last trip.

Quickly turning into the house, she tried to avoid thinking about her brother and her regrets. Lacey was walking back towards her from the back of a long hallway, rubbing her hands together for warmth.

Just then, both men walked onto the front porch and shook their heads like dogs, shaking the rain from their hair. They wiped their feet on the wire mat before crossing into the entryway.

Megan noted that their faces were very similar, yet she could see subtle differences in the men. Their height and weight for one. Iian was slightly taller, with a broader build. And although the brothers shared the same gorgeous eyes, it was the depth of the one brother's that captured her attention again.

"Megan, this is my older brother, Todd," Lacey said from behind her.

Todd nodded his hello and looked at her, causing warmth to spread throughout her.

"It's chilly in here. Will you please start a fire in the living room before the guests arrive?" Lacey asked him.

Again, a nod was his only reply, and then he turned and went into the dark room to the right without saying a word.

"Iian," Lacey said and signed along, "please take those up to Matt's room and start a fire up there."

Lacey walked away, turning on lights as she went. Iian jogged up the curved staircase that sat to the left of the entryway. He had her suitcase in one arm like it weighed nothing and had thrown her overnight bag over his shoulder. It had taken all of her strength to drag those two bags through the airport that morning. His hair was still dripping wet and he was humming to himself. Humming? Megan thought.

As everyone bustled around, starting fires and turning on lights, Megan stood in the main entryway. She felt useless all over again. Here she was standing in her brother's home, letting strangers take care of her. Hadn't she promised herself that she would take care of herself from now on? But she was so tired. She didn't think that letting these people help her out for one night would hurt.

Lacey came back into the entryway. "Come on, let's get you out of that wet coat." Lacey reached for the rain jacket as Megan flinched away. Slowly Lacey's hands returned to her side.

"I'm sorry," Megan began, looking down at her hands, not wanting to look Lacey in the eyes. "I'm just a bit jumpy and tired I suppose." She tried to smile. How could she explain she didn't like to be touched?

"No need to apologize," Lacey said, warmly. "You must be overwhelmed. I'm sure a bit hungry by now, too. At any rate, people will start arriving any minute, and I'm sure there will be lots of food." As Lacey finished those words, the doorbell rang. "Go on in and have a seat by the fire. I'll take care of this."

Lacey pointed Megan in the direction of the two French doors that Todd had disappeared through earlier. Slowly walking towards them, Megan listened as Lacey greeted a group of people. Not really wanting to deal with anyone yet, she slipped inside the softly lit room and sighed as she rested against the wall.

Todd was across the room, bent over a pile of

wood in the fireplace, blowing on flames that had started on some crumpled papers. He'd removed his leather jacket, and she noticed that he was wearing a white dress shirt that was stretched taut over his muscular arms. *Powerful* was the word that came to her mind. She was nervous around powerful, so instead of walking over to the warmth of the fire, she turned back towards the doorway and watched Lacey greet everyone.

She was about to walk out to the hall and try to find the kitchen, when she felt hands lightly placed on her shoulders. Out of reflex, she jumped and spun around, her hand raised in defense.

"Easy," Todd murmured. "Let me take your coat; you're soaking wet." He held his hands out as one would to a wounded animal.

Blushing, she said, "I'm sorry. You startled me." She hung her head and turned around so that he wouldn't see her face turning red. Her heart was racing and her hands started shaking. It still affected her, being touched.

Gently, he helped her out of her jacket, being extra careful around her right arm. He hung it next to his coat on an oak rack by the door. When he noticed Lacey watching from the doorway, he said to her, "She can eat by the fire. She's frozen."

Lacey nodded in agreement. "There's a TV tray over in the corner. Go on, I'll bring a plate of food in once it's heated."

Father Michael had just walked into the house and was standing in the doorway with a few other people. Todd nodded to them then quickly walked her back into the living room under several watchful eyes. His hand gently cupped her good elbow.

Megan followed him back towards the fireplace where the room was warmer. She held her hand out towards the fire. She hadn't realized how freezing she was until the warmth hit her, causing her hand to tingle.

"I'm sorry. I didn't realize how cold I was until now," she said nervously to the room. She knew Todd was still behind her but didn't wanted to turn and look at him just yet. Closing her eyes, she let out the breath she'd been holding since he'd touched her. She was nervous around him, around men. When he touched her, however feather light it was, it was like a power surge rushing through her body. She'd been avoiding getting close to anyone for so long that she knew she was out of practice. Taking a deep breath, she turned to the quiet room.

"You have his eyes." He interrupted her thoughts. He stood right inside the doors, his hands buried deep in his pockets as he watched her.

Megan was about to say something, anything, but just then Iian came into the room with a smile on his face. He stopped and took one look at his brother and then at her and signed something quickly to Todd. She wasn't sure what he said, but

Todd gave his brother a frustrated look and then walked out of the room without saying a word to either of them.

Iian walked over to her and took her hand in his and said in a rich, warm voice, "Megan, I am very sorry about Matt."

Gasping, she realized she wasn't aware he could speak.

He smiled slightly. "I can speak. I lost my hearing in an accident when I was eighteen. I don't do it very often; my brother and sister say I have the most annoying voice."

She could hear the little blunders he made with his voice, as if he was out of practice. But he had such a rich, deep voice, so much like his brother's.

Speaking slowly and making sure to keep her face directed at his, she said, "You have a wonderful voice, rich and warm. Thank you for taking care of my luggage and starting a fire upstairs."

He smiled, while still holding her hand in his warm one. "You're chilled. Come over and sit down." He pulled her towards a dark-colored couch near the fireplace. "Lacey is still greeting people, but I'm sure you'll have a plate of food in front of you in no time. I'll sit with you and keep you company until then."

Back in the kitchen, Todd was helping his sister with the food, but his mind was back in the living room. He'd guessed by the look in Megan's eyes and the way she had jumped at his light touch that someone had hurt her, and recently too. The look on her face was heartbreaking, and he didn't care to see it on Matt's little sister. He was glad she'd turned away when she had, so she couldn't see the sadness and anger that had come into his eyes. Had Matt known this was going on? What she'd been going through? He didn't think so, but that didn't keep him from wanting to hunt someone down for the pain they had caused her.

His sister had seen the look on his face; she always saw everything. She had shaken her head at him and discreetly signed to him not to look so serious, that he might scare her. He'd quickly dropped his eyes and hidden it. He'd been so concerned about her, he hadn't even realized that his face had shown it.

Earlier, he'd watched Megan when she'd gone to the fire. She had started to relax and had rolled her shoulders, showing him a hint of her long white neck. He'd felt a flash of desire so strong that he had winced. That was when Iian had entered the room and signed for him not to look so serious. Was he that serious of a person that both his siblings had to warn him about it in one day? He didn't want to scare Megan, but he couldn't control the way his emotions played out on his face.

His brother and sister had a way of seeing things for what they were, which always annoyed him. At this point, he couldn't even muster up enough strength to go in there and talk with his brother about his feelings. He knew he wouldn't get anywhere talking about it with Lacey, but he could at least hold his own with Iian.

Hearing people roam about the house, he could just imagine Iian and Megan in the other room talking. His brother had a way of making women feel very comfortable and at ease. Thinking about them getting together, he realized that maybe he did have enough strength to go talk to his brother about his feelings.

As he walked towards the kitchen door to go and do just that, Lacey stopped him with one word. "Don't."

He turned to her ready to argue, but she only smiled at him.

Quickly, he let his breath out in a loud puff.

"How is it that you can defuse any situation with that smile?" he said, pulling her into a hug. "You drive me nuts."

She sighed and hugged him back, resting her head on his chest. "Give her time, Todd. Let Iian talk to her a while. She's going to need to trust us. She's had it hard." Taking a deep breath and a step back, she grabbed a plate of food and handed it to him. "Now, go take this to her, and no more strange looks!" She smiled as she pushed him out the door.

Every bone in his body said that his sister was right, but his blood was boiling so hot he wanted answers. Matt had been like a brother to him, not just his best friend. What hurt Matt, hurt him. He missed his friend and felt sad, angry, and lost about his death. He knew Matt would've wanted them to take care of Megan and so he was going to make sure she was taken care of, period.

He knew that his brother and sister felt the same way about her as he did. Megan was family now. But he couldn't deny the quick pull he'd felt when he looked into those sea green eyes of hers.

Books in the West Series by Jill Sanders

Other books by Jill Sanders

The Pride Series
Finding Pride
Discovering Pride
Returning Pride
Lasting Pride
Serving Pride
Red Hot Christmas
My Sweet Valentine
Return To Me
Rescue Me

The Secret Series
Secret Seduction
Secret Pleasure
Secret Guardian
Secret Passions
Secret Identity
Secret Sauce

The West Series
Loving Lauren
Taming Alex
Holding Haley
Missy's Moment
Breaking Travis
Roping Ryan
Wild Bride
Corey's Catch

The Grayton Series
Last Resort
Someday Beach
Rip Current
In Too Deep
Swept Away

Lucky Series
Unlucky In Love
Sweet Resolve

Silver Cove Series
Silver Lining

For a complete list of books: http://jillsanders.com

This is a work of fiction. Names, characters, places and incidents either are the product of the author's imagination or are used fictitiously, and any resemblance to actual persons, living or dead, business establishments, events or locales is entirely coincidental.

TESSA'S TURN
DIGITAL ISBN: 978-1-942896-66-1
PRINT ISBN: 978-1-942896-67-8

About the Author

 Jill Sanders is *The New York Times* and *USA Today* bestselling author of the Pride, Secret, West, Grayton, Lucky Series, and Silver Cove romance novels. She continues to lure new readers with her sweet and sexy stories. Her books are available in every English-speaking country as audiobooks and are now being translated into different languages.

Born as an identical twin to a large family, she was raised in the Pacific Northwest and later relocated to Colorado for college and a successful IT career before discovering her talent as a writer. She now makes her home along the Emerald Coast in Florida where she enjoys the beach, hiking, swimming, wine-tasting, and of course writing.

Connect with Jill on Facebook: http://fb.com/JillSandersBooks

Twitter: @JillMSanders or visit her Web site at http://JillSanders.com

CPSIA information can be obtained
at www.ICGtesting.com
Printed in the USA
FSOW02n0107290118
43904FS

9 781942 896678